Dreams On Ice

GIRLS ONLY (GO!)

Dreams on Ice
Only the Best
A Perfect Match
Reach for the Stars

GIRLS GO ONLY!

Dreams On Ice

BEVERLY LEWIS

BETHANY HOUSE PUBLISHERS
MINNEAPOLIS, MINNESOTA 55438

Published by Bethany House Publishers
A Ministry of Bethany Fellowship International
11400 Hampshire Avenue South
Minneapolis, Minnesota 55438
www.bethanyhouse.com

Printed in the United States of America by
Bethany Press International, Minneapolis, Minnesota 55438

ISBN 0–7642–2058–6

For
Heidi Van Wieren,
devoted to her own ice dreams.

Author's Note

Special thanks to the U.S. Figure Skating Association and the U.S. Olympic Committee for research assistance. Also, hugs to Heidi Van Wieren, who answered all my questions about skating competitions, programs, judging, and jumps. And to each of my readers who asked me to please write another series—*for girls only*—thanks for your encouragment and wonderful letters!

BEVERLY LEWIS is the bestselling author of over fifty books, including the popular CUL-DE-SAC KIDS and SUMMERHILL SECRETS series, and her adult fiction series, THE HERITAGE OF LANCASTER COUNTY. Her *Cows in the House* picture book is a rollicking Thai folktale for all ages. She and her husband have three children, as well as two snails, Fred and Fran, and make their home in Colorado, within miles of the Olympic Training Center, headquarters for the U.S. Olympic Committee.

CHAPTER

Olivia Hudson pushed off toward center ice. Gaining speed, she skated a smooth, backward glide across the practice rink—the setup for her next move. She dug her toe pick hard into the slick surface.

Whoosh!

She leaped high into the air, tightening her arms against her body as she whirled around. A single skate met the ice on the back outside edge—the perfect landing for a super double flip.

"Excellent, Livvy!" Coach Elena Dimitri called from the sidelines.

Livvy clenched her hands in triumph, circling the arena. "I did it!" she shouted. Then, extending her left leg, she moved to a graceful spiral glide.

After a short cooling-down period, Livvy took her ten-minute break. "My timing's still off," she moaned.

Elena touched Livvy's shoulder. "Don't be too hard on

yourself. We'll get your sparkle back . . . *and* your confidence. You'll see."

I hope she's right, Livvy thought, hurrying off to get a drink.

Two heartbreaking months had passed since the coolest mom in history had lost her battle with leukemia. Livvy would never forget that June night, standing next to the hospital bed and holding the soft, dear hand. Never, ever would she accept the unbearable moment when she said her tearful farewell.

Yet here she was, anticipating her regular forty-minute skating session, trying her best to go on with life.

When she returned to the rink, she inhaled deeply, ready to go to work on her technique. "I need more practice on my flips," Livvy said.

"Triples this time," Elena insisted.

Livvy paused a moment on the mat-lined walkway. "C'mon, now . . . *focus!*" she told herself, stepping onto the ice.

She skated backward for the setup. But she entered the jump too slowly and tilted off balance, losing her footing on the landing.

"Rats!" she muttered and got up to try again.

She waited a bit longer into the glide before attempting the jump. But her concentration was off, and she fell to the ice.

I've landed this a thousand times, she told herself. *I can do this!*

Promptly, she got up and brushed the frost off her leg.

At eleven, going on twelve, Livvy knew enough not to be

discouraged over one bad skating session. Often, she'd had to force her brain to focus on winning thoughts, even at her advanced novice stage. Only one step away from juniors!

"I believe in you," her mom had always said. The encouraging words echoed in her memory. Loud and clear.

Since her preschool days, Livvy had been attending group skating classes near Riverdale, the close-knit Chicago suburb she called home. And Mom never missed a practice. *"Keep smiling!"* she would call from the stands.

Skating was the best part of the day. Any day. Livvy would rather skate than sleep, even on a summer Saturday. She'd hopped out of bed at the first musical strains of the clock radio. Even though it might've seemed like the middle of the night to the rest of the neighborhood, she hurried to the kitchen for her usual cereal, fruit, and juice. Cold (and lonely) breakfasts were common these days. Gone were the amazing breakfast specialties Mom often prepared: whole-grain waffles or homemade cereals.

Sighing, she skimmed the rink. "Oh, Mom, I wish you were still alive. I *need* you." She glanced at the bleachers—Mom's old spot—and thought about this one-sided dialogue. *Dad would probably be upset if he knew*, she thought.

Her father was a freelance artist—and totally occupied with deadlines. Definitely, he'd frown on her endless murmurings to her dead mother. She was absolutely sure he would, because after the funeral he'd stopped talking about Livvy's mom. He didn't even mention her name anymore.

Elena had said not to worry. "Your father is facing grief his own way. He's a sensitive man. He'll learn to cope . . . eventually."

It seemed like a reasonable explanation at the time. But now—two months later—her dad was still silent. A dismal kind of silence that frightened her. Worse than that, she felt terribly alone in the world. Alone and wondering how she could possibly reach her skating goals without the support of a parent who understood her Olympic dreams.

On top of everything else, money was tight. Especially after her mom's health declined so quickly and the hospital bills started pouring in. She honestly wondered if they could even afford a new outfit for the Summer Ice Revue—in just ten days!

Livvy wished with all her heart she could talk certain things over with her dad. She'd outgrown her old costumes, for one thing. And she wished he'd show even the slightest interest in her skating. Or maybe just take her to practice sessions once in a while. Things like that.

But she knew his broken heart was stuck in the past, in those wonderful Mom-filled days before everything changed . . . for the worse.

"Try again, Livvy!" Elena's voice always gave her the strength to start over.

Livvy bit her lip. *I won't give up . . . ever!*

Everything she had went into the next setup—her speed and every ounce of strength. She dug the toe pick hard and lifted her body up, up, high off the surface of the rink.

For three rapid rotations, she was flying. But the landing was off.

And Livvy fell again.

CHAPTER 2

Livvy dropped her skate bag on the living room floor. "Dad, I'm home!" she called, wandering through the house. She found him in the family room, reading the evening paper.

He looked up only briefly. "Hi, Liv. Good day?"

"Horrible." She dropped into the chair that had been her mother's favorite—a cozy, old wingback—and stared at her tall, slender dad. He seemed to be growing thinner by the day. "I'm really worried," she said softly.

His eyebrows arched as he peered over the paper. "Are you all right?"

"I'm worried about *you*," she answered.

"Olivia, let's not—"

"We *need* to talk."

He sighed and folded the newspaper. Leaning back against the sofa, his green eyes were serious, his lanky arms folded tightly against his chest.

"You aren't yourself." Livvy felt her heart pounding like a snare drum. "You're tired all the time, Daddy. And you don't eat enough."

Without speaking, he ran his fingers slowly through his thick, dark hair. The silence unnerved her.

"I think I know what's wrong." Her throat felt tight. Achy. "I think I understand . . . because I miss Mom, too. I miss her more than ever."

He blinked repeatedly, his gaze clearly fixed on her. It would do no good to continue. The conversation was going nowhere. Same as all the other times.

Frustrated, she stood up to leave, but his startling words stopped her. "I'm thinking of moving." He paused for a moment. "There's a mountain town in Colorado . . . not too far from Colorado Springs. I'd like to move us there before school starts."

Move?

Livvy froze. This was her home—Dad's too. And Mom's! What was he thinking?

"We can't . . . move, Daddy." She stopped short of crying. There were hundreds of reasons for them to stay. Sensible reasons—more than she could count. But one of the best reasons on earth was her skating coach. How could she possibly leave the woman who'd brought her through all the early competitions of her life? Elena, who had instructed her and cheered her on all the way to novice level—incredible for Livvy's age.

She shook her head, hair swirling against her face. Standing, she faced her father. "How can you even think of doing this to me? You're going to ruin my life!"

He frowned, then a helpless look clouded his face. "Perhaps we should consider having you stay here in Riverdale. Grandma Hudson has an extra bedroom."

She could hardly believe her ears. Her father was going to abandon her? Move halfway across the United States? Hand her off to Grandma?

Livvy fought back tears and the throbbing lump in her throat. She wanted him to say he could never leave without her, that he didn't want to move anywhere without his baby girl. Or . . . no, she wanted him to say he wasn't really going to move. Let her grow up in Riverdale, let her finish middle school and later high school. All because of her skating goals. *That's* what she wanted him to say.

"We belong here," she managed to squeak out. "You know it, and so do I."

He stared at the ceiling, his feet restless on the floor. "A change would do us both good" came the hollow-sounding reply.

"A change? Isn't losing Mom enough of a change for one summer?" Livvy was immediately filled with regret. Her dad was obviously hurting, and she knew it by the dismal look on his ashen face. "I shouldn't have said that. I'm sorry, Daddy."

"No . . . no. Maybe you're right." He was studying her now. "It's just that, well, this house . . . this . . ." He was faltering, reaching for the paper again.

"I know, Dad. I know." She looked around the room at her mother's porcelain angel collection with Bible verses inscribed on each one. At the accent candles in different shapes and sizes: hearts, stars, cubes, and tapers. Everything reminded her of what they'd lost. Everything, right down to the way the drapes were pulled over with a fashionable gold clip.

Later, in her room, Livvy stood with her face next to her cockatiel's cage. Coco blinked his tiny eyes. "Hi, cutie-bird," she whispered, staring at his adorable white body and bright yellow head.

"Coco . . . cutie-bird" came the low-pitched voice.

"You're one crazy parrot." She puckered her lips to send kisses.

Coco didn't send any back. Not this time. He was playing hard to get.

"Okay, have it your way." She turned her back on purpose.

"Way . . . way crazy!" Coco repeated the words ten or more times without stopping.

Finally Livvy faced him again and shushed him. "Better be quiet now. Dad's in a lousy mood." She waved her pointer finger close to the cage. "And so am I."

"Ha . . . ha . . . ha . . . quiet!" was the annoying reply.

"Okay for you. If you won't behave, I'll just have to ignore you. Or cover up your cage for the rest of the day." It was a threat, nothing more. But she turned and shuffled across the room.

Gazing out the window, her thoughts flew to her dad. "He's not thinking clearly," she murmured, watching a flock of birds wing their way from tree to tree. "He's lost without Mom. . . ."

Nearly a year ago, right after she and her mother had become Christians, Livvy began to worry about her dad's disinterest in God and church. He seemed so puzzled about everything. Like he was searching his heart for answers to what had happened to his cozy, unbelieving family.

She understood his present sadness and loss, but this unexpected talk of moving to Colorado . . . What was *that* about?

When Coco didn't chatter back one of his favorite words, Livvy was surprised. Thankful, though. She needed some space, some time to think. Should she go with her dad? Or stay and seriously pursue her skating goals?

Livvy sighed and sat at her desk, leaning on her elbows. A small picture of her mother smiled back at her. "What should I do, Mom?" she asked the photo.

Asking the Lord would've made more sense, she knew. But these days it was too painful to pray. Why *had* God taken her mother at such a young age?

Pulling open the narrow drawer in the center of her desk, she found her stationery. Her Colorado pen pal— Jenna Song—was always a super sounding board. And Jenna was an avid letter writer. Same as Livvy. The girls might've been email addicts, but neither of them had access to a computer. Livvy's dad's state-of-the-art computer and printer were always in use.

Twirling a ballpoint pen between her fingers, Livvy eyed the bulletin board above her desk. There, centered among pictures of Tara Lipinski and Michelle Kwan, skating souvenirs, and ticket stubs, was Jenna. Beautifully Korean, with flawless olive skin, deep brown eyes, and dark hair down to her waist. Jenna prided herself in being "absolutely American." That's how she'd introduced herself in the first letter three months ago.

Jenna was also a minister's daughter, but she didn't flaunt it like some kids might. She *did* talk about God in her letters sometimes. Once, when Livvy had confided in her about her mother's cancer, Jenna had written back, promising to pray.

Remembering this, Livvy decided to go ahead and share her gloomy news. Coco twittered in the cage behind her, and Livvy took a deep breath and began to write.

August 12
Dear Jenna,

Hi again! Did you place at your gymnastics meet last weekend in Denver? I hope you were psyched for it and did super great.

Well, I hate to write this, but I have some upsetting news. My dad has this horrible idea. He wants to move. Can you believe it? We've lived here my WHOLE life. And there's the big problem of leaving my skating friends—AND my skating coach. I simply couldn't exist without Elena, you know.

I overheard Daddy telling Grandma Hudson that he plans to move to Alpine Lake, somewhere in Colorado. Sounds like Podunk, USA, to me. Any idea where it is? I wonder if it's close to your town. I'll have to check the map.

If I stayed here I could live with Grandma and keep

training with Elena. Then I'd end up missing BOTH my parents. So if I move with Dad, I might as well kiss my skating goals good-bye. No matter what I choose, I lose!

I wish Dad would stay put for another couple of years, then maybe I'd have a chance at junior-level competition. I can tell you all this, Jen, because we're a lot alike.

Sorry about not sending you a picture of me yet. Maybe we'll meet each other face-to-face sometime soon. (That's IF I decide to move with Dad.) Getting to meet you in person would be the only good thing about leaving Riverdale.

> *Write soon!*
> *Love ya,*
> *Livvy*

She folded her letter, then undressed for bed. After draping Coco's cage for the night, Livvy set her clock radio for 5:00 A.M.

She slipped into bed and reached to turn out the light on the lamp table. "Night-night, Coco," she whispered.

The parrot replied, "Night-night."

Livvy was thrilled to own a peculiar pet like Coco. Crazy and talkative as he was, she adored him. It had been her mother's idea to buy the exotic pet in the first place. Now Coco was one more link to her perfect past.

The room was too hot for bedcovers, so Livvy lay there in her shortie pajamas, enjoying the breeze from the window. Part of the moon shone through the curtains, casting a white light on the ice skater figurine on her bookcase. The statuette was last year's birthday gift. By far the best present ever. Livvy was sure she knew which of her parents had purchased it.

"How can I skate . . . or live . . . without you, Mom?" she whispered into the stillness. "I miss you something awful."

CHAPTER 3

The flap of a screen door startled her awake. Livvy sat up in bed and squinted at the clock.

4:32 A.M.

She crawled out of bed and stumbled to the window. Below her, on the back porch step, sat her father.

What's he doing up? she wondered.

This was so unlike him. Especially because he often stayed up past midnight working on new illustrations and trying out new color combinations. The creative side of his brain switched on at night like a light bulb.

On several occasions Livvy had wandered into his studio late, only to find him boring a hole in a canvas with his eyes, a brush poised in midair . . . usually talking to himself or to the painted subject.

She stared at him through the window, her thoughts soaring. Slowly, she began to get her hopes up. Way up.

Maybe, just maybe, Dad was planning to surprise her—take her to skating for once!

Too excited to sleep again, she took a shower and dressed for practice. *Wait'll I write Jenna about this*, she thought, wishing she hadn't already sealed the envelope.

Finding it, she toyed with the notion of including a big, fat P.S. on the back. But no, she wouldn't want anyone to read her comment. Least of all Dad.

She would wait and send another note. After practice would be a good time. She'd tell Jenna all about her dad's first visit to the rink, watching her practice her jumps and spins. He would observe her stamina training . . . her technique study. Everything! This was too good to be true!

Livvy brushed her auburn hair back into a quick ponytail. She studied her full bangs in the mirror, wondering if she should let them grow out so she could wear her hair pulled back, like Michelle Kwan. Or trim them and make them fluffier, like Tara Lipinski.

She set her hairbrush back on the dresser, unable to decide about a new look. Standing in front of the mirror, her eyes fell on another framed picture of her mother. Her all-time favorite.

Holding the familiar image up to her face, she compared the picture to herself. "Mom and I actually looked like sisters . . . almost." Having made this discovery, her tears threatened to spill over.

Quickly, she placed the picture back on the dresser. Her stomach rumbled loudly, and she hurried downstairs to the kitchen. Too much thinking made her super hungry, but before she opened the cereal box, she peered out the back door.

Dad was nowhere to be seen.

Her heart sank as she poured milk over the cereal. Livvy knew as sure as she was Olivia Kay Hudson that her dad had probably gone back to bed. He wouldn't be available to take her to the rink. Not today.

Probably not ever.

She would have to catch a ride with a skating friend. Once again, she was on her own.

After lunch, Livvy dashed to her bedroom and tore open her letter to Jenna. She sat at her desk and wrote the longest P.S. ever.

She began by explaining how miserable she felt. How totally disappointed . . .

> *P.S. My dad's in the blackest cloud ever! He hardly even paid attention when I pleaded with him today. About NOT moving, that is. He's determined to start a new life somewhere else. Somewhere far away from all our happy memories.*
>
> *Doesn't he know that a part of Mom will always go with him no matter where he ends up?*
>
> *Oh, Jenna, you should've seen my coach's face when I told her Dad wants to move. She looked absolutely ill. And I felt as sick as she looked. I haven't told Dad yet, but I'm honestly thinking of staying here with my grandma. I can't throw away everything I've ever worked for. Can I?*

Livvy found another envelope in her skinny desk drawer

and rewrote the address. Without mangling the self-adhesive stamp, she removed it from the old envelope. She secured it to the new envelope with a thump of her fist.

Before mailing her letter, she took time to clean the bottom of Coco's cage. She also gave her parrot some fresh water and more food. "Say 'thank you, Livvy,' " she prompted him.

"Coco, cutie-bird." He turned his neck to preen his feathers.

"No, say 'thank you,' " she repeated.

"Cutie Livvy" came the unexpected reply.

She couldn't help but smile. "You're just too much, you know?"

"Too much . . . too much."

"I'm leaving now. Bye!" She closed her bedroom door, but Coco kept chitter-chattering.

Letter in hand, Livvy hurried down the hall to her dad's studio. She stopped to peek inside, expecting to see him consumed in the latest art project.

Instead, she found him draped over the sketching table, snoozing. Soft music, featuring flowing water and chirping birds mingled with guitar melodies, played in the background. The music and the wilderness sounds were relaxing. No wonder he was sound asleep in the middle of the afternoon.

Tiptoeing inside, Livvy went to stand near his chair. She looked down on her grieving father and noticed dark circles under his eyes. And his face seemed horribly pale.

Oh, Daddy, I love you, she thought and felt her heart breaking all over again. *Whatever happens to my skating dreams, even if I have to give it all up, I can't let you go to Colorado. Not without me!*

CHAPTER

It was a cloudy Saturday. Just two more days before doors opened at Alpine Lake Middle School. The *only* middle school in town.

Big whoop.

Ordinarily, Livvy would be practicing her routines on a day like this. Back in first-class Chicago! But she busied herself with cleaning and organizing her new room, trying to shove away thoughts of future competitions. Of skating buddies and the best coach in the world.

Her dreams had been put on hold. She'd even missed out on the Summer Ice Revue—something she'd worked for all year. But worst of all, she'd had to leave Elena behind. No coach . . . no skating career. Yet she couldn't blame anyone but herself for landing here in Podunk. A place precisely in the middle of nowhere!

The realtor had shown them only three houses. All of them run-down Victorians. One far worse than the others.

Amazingly, her dad had purchased the most hopeless of the bunch. He said he was going to "remodel the seventies away" and recapture the heart of the house.

Whatever that means, Livvy had thought at the time.

So here she was rattling around in an old fixer-upper, awaking each morning to pounding and sawing. "Dad's taking his misery out on this poor old house," Livvy informed her parrot.

"Poor house" came the answer.

"Right, the *poorhouse* is exactly where we're gonna end up."

"End up . . . end up."

Livvy laughed and blew kisses to Coco. "Try to behave yourself today. Is that possible? Because I'm going school shopping."

"Missing Liv . . . missing Liv . . ."

She shook her head, wondering how Coco had gotten so smart. She'd worked with him repeatedly their first years together. As a result, he could carry on like a chicken, sneeze like a human, and repeat most any phrase she'd ever taught him. But sometimes he actually seemed to think for himself. Uncanny. Never a dull moment with Coco.

At least she had *one* friend in town!

The shops on the edge of Alpine Lake were the poorest excuse for a mall Livvy had ever seen. She found herself buying school supplies at a drugstore, of all places!

When she'd checked off her list and paid for her supplies,

she wandered over to another shop—the Cloth Mill. There she searched through bolts of bright-colored fabric and packages of sparkly sequins.

"May I help you?" a cheerful clerk asked.

"Just looking, thanks."

The woman chuckled a bit, her turquoise bracelet jangling. "Please, feel free to look around. And take all the time you need. We have plenty of markdowns this weekend."

"Okay, I'll look."

Pausing, the clerk asked, "Are you from the Midwest somewhere?"

"Chicago," she said proudly.

The woman clicked her fingers. "I thought so!"

"Really?" Livvy was surprised. "Do I have an accent?"

"I never would've guessed, except that I have some cousins who live back there. You sound just like them."

Livvy felt completely comfortable telling the clerk that she and her father had just moved to Alpine Lake. "It's a first for me . . . moving someplace new."

"Well, let me be the first to welcome you to the prettiest place on earth."

Easy for her to say. Livvy forced a smile.

"Why so glum? Our town's full of wonderful folks, you'll see."

"I'm sure it is." Quickly, she filled the clerk in on her biggest worry. "It's just that I'm an ice skater . . . without a coach."

"Oh, that *is* a problem." The woman's eyes were kind and sincere. "You'll just have to practice on the mall skating rink, I guess."

"There's a rink *here*?"

The woman nodded emphatically. "Go see for yourself." She gave easy directions. "You can't miss it."

Normally, Livvy never would have confided in a stranger like this, but the clerk had such an honest face. Like her own mother's. And there was something endearing about the way the woman's eyes focused right on her, tears glistening in the corners when Livvy told of her mother's recent death.

"Oh, I'm terribly sorry."

The more they talked, the more Livvy liked the well-dressed clerk. She soon discovered that the sunny Mrs. Newton was a regular volunteer at the middle school.

"Then I'll be seeing you again," Livvy said before leaving.

"Oh, you'll see me, all right!"

Livvy couldn't help but feel encouraged. Grandma Hudson had told her that "small-town folks are some of the friendliest around."

She hoped Grandma was right about *all* the people here as she headed off to check out the skating rink. Along the way, she noticed several other girls shopping with their moms.

Sighing, she hated the thought of trying to survive middle school and beyond without Mom. She tried not to gawk but felt super envious and sad. Very sad.

Livvy scurried off, leaving the girls and their mothers behind. She located the mall rink quickly. It was situated in the middle of the small emporium. Tall trees with twinkling white lights dotted the area around the rink.

"Super stuff," she said to herself.

Walking all the way around, she remembered every ice

skating event she and her mom had attended. Always together. With everything in her, she hoped someday she
could get back on track with skating. She'd have to go
through the hassle of finding a new coach to regain what
she'd already lost. By not training every single day, she could
lose some of the long-practiced, perfected spirals, spins, and
jumps.

Every day!

It would take forever to get back her agility and strength.
In more ways than one, Livvy's dreams were on ice. . . .

GO CHAPTER 5

"But, Dad, you *promised*!"

Her father looked up from a pile of lumber and sanding tools in what had been their living room. He surveyed the mess. "Sorry, Liv. I didn't realize this project would take so long. Can we surprise your pen pal another weekend?"

"Like when? *Next* Sunday?"

"That's a good possibility."

His answer was too uncertain. Here they were, only one hour's drive away from her pen pal! They'd checked out the distance on the map. And now her dad was changing his mind and calling off the trip.

She slumped onto the bottom step, its wood stripped bare of stain. "I was living for today . . . to finally meet Jenna," she said softly. "I don't know anyone around here."

"You know *me*." Her father's face was caked with sawdust, almost comically so.

But she refused to laugh. He'd let her down, and she felt

like pouting or worse. "This town is so boring."

"Well, if you want something exciting to do, *here*." He held out the sander. "I could use a little help."

He had a point. So she spent her entire afternoon helping with her dad's latest art project—remodeling their horrid house! Livvy sanded woodwork—baseboards and trim around doorways—till she thought her arm would keep vibrating by itself. Even after the sander was turned off!

When it was time for supper, she talked her dad into driving them to the mall for burgers. "There's a skating rink in the middle of the shops," she said. It was the first she'd breathed a word of her discovery.

"There's a skating rink in a boring town like this?" he teased.

Livvy wished he would show some real excitement. For a change. "There are skaters everywhere in this world," she insisted. *"Everywhere*. You can't get away from rinks and skaters . . . no matter where we live."

He shrugged. Clearly, he wasn't interested.

But Livvy had an idea. She would take her skates along and try out the ice, and her dad would watch. He'd have to!

She wouldn't say a thing about her plan. Not one word.

While her dad shaved and showered, she hid her skate bag in the backseat of the car. Super cool! This was the moment she'd been waiting for.

An hour later, Livvy and her dad were waiting in line at the only fast-food place in town. "What're you gonna order?" she asked, hoping that his appetite might be returning to normal.

"Probably a milk shake."

"Daddy! You've been working hard all day. You need something *real* to eat."

He chortled. "Real, eh?"

"You know what I mean. I don't want you to fade away to nothing. Please, won't you eat a sandwich?"

His cheeks flinched, and for the first time in weeks he put his arm around her. "I'll think about it, kiddo."

When they got up to the window, she was pleased to hear her dad order a cheeseburger and fries. Her hopes were high for a similar response to her personal skating revue. If she could just divert his attention long enough to retrieve her skates from the car, lace up, and claim center ice.

That's when she thought of talkative Mrs. Newton at the fabric shop. "Can we window shop a little?" she asked as they located a table for two.

Her father groaned at the request. "You know how shopping affects me." He began to massage his temples. "I feel a migraine coming on."

"We'll just look, I promise."

He shook his head as if to say, "This is hopeless."

"Honest, Dad. I won't buy a thing!"

She waited, but he said no more. Encouraged, she assumed that his silence was a yes. She could hardly wait. "The Cloth Mill's nearby. It's a fabric shop."

"Fabric?"

"You know, to make outfits."

He frowned. "What outfits?"

"New school clothes, for one." She didn't dare mention skating costumes. Not yet.

Nodding, he continued to nibble on his cheeseburger.

Livvy didn't want to distract him from his food. But she *did* want to get him thinking about the Cloth Mill. She could only hope that Mrs. Newton was working tonight.

"I could use some new tops for school," she said. "I made a couple last fall. Mom and I—"

"We can *afford* to buy ready-made clothing," he interrupted.

"But, Dad, I—"

"There's no need for you to sew." His voice cracked, and when he reached to crumple their trash, Livvy saw that his hand was shaking.

So her plan was shot.

She didn't say a word about the fabric store again. And she didn't bother to show him the skating rink, either.

Pointless!

CHAPTER 6

Br-r-ring!

The clock alarm jangled her awake. Livvy slammed her hand down on the turn-off button.

Ah . . . peace. She was tempted to lie back and snooze. Instead, she sat up and stretched.

Five o'clock seemed horribly early in Colorado. She had been getting up before dawn ever since grade-school days. Why was it so hard today?

Leaning back on her pillows, she stared past the tall windows at the opposite end of her spacious room. Sheer yellow curtains allowed her to see out into the blackness, thanks to the faint porch light below.

She craned her neck forward, looking and wondering. *Why is it so dark here?*

Getting up, she tiptoed to the stairs, heading to the third floor. Soon it would be the studio loft. Once her dad finished the main part of the house, he planned to do some major work on his artist's getaway. Private and quaint, it was the ideal spot for his creativity.

She noticed his wall clock, the shape of an easel. Listening, she could hear its gentle clicking.

5:07 A.M. Same time as her clock.

Hurrying back to her room, she stood at the window. A dense cloud cover was the reason for the darkness. It was impossible for the sun to shine through. The weather matched her mood. This was to be her first skating day in Podunk town. A skating session on her own. Could she pull it off?

The mini mall was nearly deserted, except for a few early-morning walkers. Mostly older people, she guessed.

While doing her stretching exercises, she caught sight of two women. They looked closer to her mother's age than the others and chattered almost as fast as her cockatiel. But they didn't notice Livvy near the rink. They never paused to say "Good morning."

"Hello," she called just to see if they'd wave or greet her. They turned only briefly and smiled but kept going, their arms moving almost as fast as their trim legs.

"Looks like Mrs. Newton was only half right about the people here," she mumbled as she stepped onto the ice.

Slowly, Livvy's legs began to warm up. She focused on the perimeters of the rink, eyeing it for size. Then around and around she skated. The delicate smoothness under her blades made her homesick for Elena . . . for her skating pals in Chicago. But she had to get the feel of this rink. Not Olympic size, but better than nothing.

The festive white lights in the trees surrounding the rink blurred as she sped up. Before ever attempting a jump, she practiced a long spiral, followed by a couple of sit spins.

I still have it, she thought. *I know I do!*

She remembered the thrill of competing at regionals as a novice last November. Her mother had made the trip to Michigan even though the chemo treatments had left her terribly weak. They'd hugged hard after Livvy's free-skate program. And Elena was there, all smiles, waiting for the judges' scoring.

The announcer's words rang in her ears. *"Second place goes to Olivia Hudson from Illinois."*

Super cool! She was on her way.

"This one's for you," she'd told her mom.

"No . . . no. You deserve every bit of it, kiddo." Tears of joy streamed down her mother's cheeks.

"Mom, please don't cry." Livvy had to fight back her own tears.

Please don't cry. . . .

The gentle swoosh of her skates brought her back to the present. She would allow herself only a twenty-minute workout today. Wisely, she knew she'd have to take things slowly. Steady too.

But Elena would be proud. Livvy was actually pacing herself . . . and without a coach!

In no time, though, her legs began to feel like rubber. Time to quit. No sense pushing herself too hard, especially on the first day of the school year. Besides, she had three long blocks to walk home.

Tired and a bit winded from the high altitude, Livvy hurried down the sidewalk toward the gray-and-white Victorian. The sun was making its first appearance as she walked the final block. Long pink wisps brushed the sky, as if an artist had splashed them up there.

"I believe in you, Livvy. . . ."

The memory of her mother's words encouraged her. And she slipped into the house unnoticed.

Quietly, she changed clothes, showered, and headed for the kitchen. There she found a pitcher of orange juice already mixed and ready to drink. "Dad's up?" she said, smiling. "No way."

A bit hungry from her early morning skate, she plopped two pieces of wheat bread into the toaster. Then she packed her lunch for school. She still hadn't gotten over the shock at seeing the teensy-weensy middle school. Even Dad had agreed it was peewee size when they'd gone to enroll her.

The building was as small as Livvy's grade school back home. In fact, Principal Seeley's office couldn't have been larger than a shoe box—at least her mom would've described it that way.

She forced a laugh, mostly to squash her fears. And she wondered about her locker partner, hoping whoever it was might be as friendly as Mrs. Newton at the Cloth Mill.

More worries filled her head. *Will the kids accept me?* she wondered. *Can a wanna-be Olympic skater fit in here?*

"Ready or not, here I come!" she announced to the bread as it flew up out of the toaster.

She heard footsteps. "Morning, Livvy."

"You're up early."

Sleepily, he opened the refrigerator. "Another long day ahead," he said, pulling out a quart of milk.

"More sanding and stuff?"

His eyes lit up. "Little by little, I'll make this house livable."

She couldn't help but grin. "We're *living* in it, aren't we?" Wiggling her fingers at him, she said, "Gotta run. The bus'll be here soon."

"Uh . . . wait a minute, kiddo."

She paused. "What is it?"

His eyes seemed to look right through her. "Must you get up so early?"

She sighed. "I *have* to skate. Every day!"

"But without a coach?" He placed his spoon in the cereal bowl, staring down at it.

"I'm doing my best on my own. A town this size . . ." She paused. Did she dare say it? Should she tell her dad what she really thought of his idea to come here?

His eyes met hers. "Are you trying to tell me there aren't any coaches in Alpine Lake?"

"Not for advanced skaters like me."

"I'm sorry, Livvy. I know it's *your* thing."

Quickly, she went to him. "You don't have to be sorry. Just please share my skating dreams with me. At least pretend you care about them." She touched his shoulder lightly. "I hated leaving Elena and all my friends. I despised it with all my heart. But I honestly think I can keep up without them . . . if I have *you!*"

Her father fidgeted and glanced at the wall clock nervously.

No comment. Her dad couldn't come up with one positive thing to say! Livvy wanted to shake him, to make him understand. Instead, she turned to go.

Her heart sank. She'd tried and failed to persuade him.

Bolting into the dining room, she passed the scraps of wood shavings and cans of stain.

Upstairs, she gathered up her three-ring binder and other school supplies, shoving them into her book bag. Before heading out the front door, she called to him. "I'm leaving now." She fought back tears. No sense letting herself cry. Not now.

"Come home right after school," he said from the kitchen.

"Can't I go to the rink for a while?"

"Be home by five o'clock. No later."

She snatched up her skate bag. Then, slinging her book bag over her shoulder, she left the house. She would never tell him that he sounded exactly like Mom just then. She would never dream of saying one word.

CHAPTER 7

Green and yellow gum wrappers were stuck all over the inside locker door next to Livvy's. Two girls in matching blue T-shirts shared the locker. One of them kept snapping her bubble gum.

"Hi," Livvy said, attempting a smile.

"Hey, you must be the new girl," said the gum chewer with enormous blue eyes.

"Unfortunately."

The girls turned away, whispering and giggling.

But she wouldn't let their cattiness discourage her. "I'm Olivia Hudson," she spoke up. "Most everyone calls me Livvy, so you can, too." She slammed her locker door a bit too hard.

The girls spun around. "Whoa, the skater's got a temper," declared the blond-haired gum chewer.

Livvy bit her tongue. "I'm not mad . . . not really."

"Could've fooled me," sassed the blonde.

"Wait a minute. How'd you know I was a skater?" Livvy asked.

The girl rolled her eyes and tilted her head coyly. "I just do."

Ignoring the comment, Livvy asked, "So . . . what's *your* name?"

"Diane Larson. Captain of the cheerleading squad."

Diane's short, plump friend set the record straight. "You were captain *last* year. And don't forget it." The petite girl smiled at Livvy. "Hi, I'm Suzy Buchanan."

"Nice to meet you," Livvy said, observing both of them. Diane was tall and wiry, with chin-length blond hair. Suzy was perky and cute, with big brown eyes and a sweet smile, her brunette hair pulled back in a ponytail.

"By the way, have either of you seen my locker partner?" she asked.

Diane and Suzy displayed total shock. "You're kidding! You don't know who you're sharing your locker with?" Diane gasped.

"All your stuff's in there, right?" Suzy asked.

Livvy felt nervous. "On second thought, maybe I'll just lug everything around with me. Till I meet her."

Promptly, she worked her combination lock again and yanked open the locker. Once again, Livvy noticed the upper shelf—lined with hot-pink carpet—as she checked out the place. An oval mirror with bright pink rickrack glued to its frame was tilted on its side. The mirror was attached to the inside of the door. "Whoever it is, she likes pink. Likes to primp, too."

"Don't we all," catty Diane remarked, popping her gum.

Suzy poked her. "Be nice, okay?"

"Whatever." And with that, Diane turned and dashed away.

"Wow, your locker's all jazzed up. That oughta tell you something," Suzy offered.

The brown-eyed girl was actually trying to help. "Hey, super," Livvy said, laughing. "She's probably a wanna-be teen model or something." She stared at the gum wrappers on Suzy's locker door. "And you must be into bubble gum. Do you sell it or just chew it?"

"Both," Suzy said, swinging her ponytail. She shoved her hand into her jeans pocket. "How many packs do you want?"

"Later, maybe."

"So who'd you get for homeroom?"

Livvy dug through her book bag and found her schedule. "Smith . . . *Mrs*. Smith."

Suzy clutched her throat and made a gagging sound.

"What's wrong?"

Suzy shifted her books. "You'll find out soon enough. Diane and I had her last year."

"So you're seventh graders?" Livvy asked.

"And proud of it."

The first bell interrupted them.

"Well, is there something I should know about Mrs. Smith before I head for homeroom?" Livvy asked.

"Just don't ever let her catch you reading or writing while she's talking. It's her pet peeve. And I'm not kidding!"

"Thanks for the hint." Livvy was glad that Suzy was so friendly. Things had started out pretty iffy.

"Hope you meet your locker pal soon," Suzy called over her shoulder.

"Thanks. Me too." Livvy pushed her skate bag in the far corner of the locker and headed for Room 123—Mrs. Smith's homeroom. She reminded herself to give her undivided attention when the teacher was talking.

No problem . . . easy as a single toe loop!

Mrs. Smith got things started by greeting students. "It's good to see so many scrubbed faces . . . and smiling ones, too!"

A nervous ripple spread through the classroom. Nobody was smiling, at least not that Livvy could see.

"Now, let's get down to important business." She gave instructions for expected behavior, including the rule about paying attention at all times. "I assign 500-word essays for students who think I'm kidding."

The teacher wrote her name on the board. "This is just in case some of you forget."

Several kids snickered, but Livvy looked straight ahead.

Attendance was taken, and a few papers were handed out. "Please take these home and have a parent sign them. Return them by Wednesday . . . two days from now."

Mrs. Smith made an announcement about cheerleading tryouts. The girls sprang to life. "Sixth-grade girls will meet in the gymnasium at seven o'clock on Friday morning, September eleventh," said the teacher. "Seventh-grade girls, immediately after school on the same day. That's nearly two weeks to get in shape."

Livvy groaned inside. Why did sixth-grade tryouts have to be so early? Too close to early-morning skate time.

She waited until the teacher finished her announcements before jotting down a note about cheerleading. She didn't want to start the year out on the wrong foot. Especially in a new school.

She observed Mrs. Smith while waiting for first-period bell. The teacher couldn't have been a day over twenty-five and was well dressed. She could've passed for a department-store clerk. Or . . . a judge at an important skating event.

Livvy shrugged the last thought away. No matter where she was, no matter what she was doing, her mind kept creeping back to skating.

During lunch period, Livvy ended up sitting alone. She was glad she'd packed her own sandwich. The meatloaf from the cafeteria looked absolutely mushy. Super ick!

Her friends back home would be choking if they could see the week's hot lunch menu. Livvy had stuffed it into her book bag—with the rest of her first-day papers.

Feeling like a stranger in alien territory, she started working on her homework. Math had always been one of her favorite subjects, so she began with the first page of problems.

Suddenly, she heard a familiar voice. "Well, hello there, Livvy."

She looked up to see Mrs. Newton. "How are you?"

"Now that you're smiling, I'm doing just fine." The woman sat across from her, fingering her charm bracelet. "How's your first day so far?"

"Oh, you know . . . being the new girl is a pain." She hated to admit that she disliked the school and the town, too. "It takes time to fit in, I guess."

"Not if you're personal friends with the cheerleading coach." Mrs. Newton was beaming, pointing to herself.

"Really? You're in charge of tryouts?"

Mrs. Newton was nodding emphatically. "I guarantee you'll be as popular as punch if you hang out with me."

Livvy closed her homework. "You said you were a school volunteer when we met at the mall. I had no idea you were the cheerleading coach."

"Stick with me, Livvy. I'll make sure you get acquainted around here. And fast."

"Hey, thanks. Such a deal."

Grinning, Mrs. Newton excused herself. "I best be heading back to the library. I'm also the librarian's assistant."

Livvy couldn't believe her ears. "You're everywhere, Mrs. Newton!"

"No place I'd rather be." She waved, her bracelet jangling. "Come see me at the mall when you practice again."

Before Livvy could stop her, Mrs. Newton was swallowed up by the cafeteria crowd. Mostly by girls vying for her attention.

So . . . Mrs. Newton had seen her skating at the mall rink. That meant she must work at the Cloth Mill *after* school hours. Livvy made a mental note to stop in and see the friendly woman there.

"Hey," Suzy Buchanan said, sliding in next to Livvy. "Are you saving a seat for me?" She blinked her eyes fast.

"Maybe."

They laughed together, which dismissed the tension a bit.

"I see you met our stunning Mrs. Newton," Suzy said.

"Yeah, she's super cool."

"You can say that again." Suzy opened her brown bag lunch and pulled out a napkin. "Have you met 'Hot Pink' yet?"

"Who?"

"Your locker partner."

"Oh, *her*. I've been back to my locker after every class but haven't seen anyone. Maybe she's absent today."

Suzy shook her head. "Whoever heard of missing school on the first day?" Neatly, she spread out her sandwich, some mini-pretzels, sliced apples, and chocolate-chip cookies. "Why don't you just hang out at your locker after school? That way you won't miss her."

"Super idea." Livvy watched her new friend first eat her sandwich, then her chips. The cookies came next, followed by three fat apple slices. "Any special reason why you save the apples for last?" she asked.

Suzy nodded, waiting to answer till she was finished chewing. "Apples clean your teeth. Did you know that?"

Livvy thought about it. "Why don't you just bring your toothbrush along and brush your teeth?"

Suzy reached into her book bag and pulled out a small zipper case. "Ta-dah!"

"You've gotta be kidding." Livvy spied a toothbrush, dental floss, and a teeny tube of toothpaste. "Looks like you're prepared for anything."

"Always!" Suzy grinned.

"So why bother eating your lunch in *any* order?" Livvy asked, noticing the remaining apple slice.

Eyebrows high, Suzy zipped the little bag shut. "Guess it's just a habit. I sorta drive people crazy that way."

"Like who?" Livvy was pretty sure she already knew.

"Diane, for one. But it's easy to annoy her, if you know what I mean."

Livvy wondered about that but played it safe and didn't ask. She thought it would be nice to talk to Suzy—friend to friend. Maybe even mention her skating goals and ask Suzy about her hobbies. Stuff like that.

She was that close to sticking her neck out and getting better acquainted when Diane Larson showed up.

"Are you trying out for cheerleader this year?" Diane asked, looking only at Suzy.

"Maybe I will, maybe I won't," Suzy sassed with a grin.

"Aw, c'mon," the taller girl said, sitting down across from them. "You have to at least try out. *Everyone* will be."

Livvy's ears perked up. "*All* the girls?"

"Well, you know." Diane seemed too eager for Suzy's reaction to make eye contact with Livvy. "So . . . *are* you?"

Suzy muttered into her brown bag, then stashed her trash inside. Turning, she looked at Livvy. "You'll come and try out, won'tcha?"

Livvy crumpled up her napkin and the sandwich bag. "Me? I doubt it."

"Why not?" Suzy persisted. "You ought to. You're tall . . . and pretty. And it looks like you're in tight with Mrs. Newton, too."

"Leave Livvy out of this," Diane blurted, her eyes flashing.

"Don't be rude," Suzy shot back.

"Don't be stupid!" Diane flounced off.

Suzy stood up, eyes pleading. "Honestly, she's totally insecure."

Livvy chuckled. "I never would've guessed."

Suzy laughed, too, and tossed her trash into the receptacle. "Hey, you're cool, Liv. See you at your locker."

Livvy felt as warm as cocoa on a winter day. Now . . . if she could just meet "Hot Pink," her mystery locker mate!

CHAPTER 8

So far, things had gone semi-okay for the first day of school. There was only one thing left to do. And Livvy was determined to do it. Even if she had to stand in front of her locker and miss the school bus, she was going to meet her locker partner!

"Any luck?" Suzy asked, gathering her books after school.

Livvy shrugged. "Beats me who she is." She surveyed the interior of her locker for the tenth time.

"Hey, wait a minute," Suzy said. "Maybe the pink carpet was glued in from last year."

Livvy didn't think so. "Except what about this snazzy mirror?" She traced the pink frame with her pointer finger. "Nobody would leave *this* behind."

"Seems like 'Hot Pink' would've stashed her books in here by now," Suzy said, peering into the locker. "Real weird, isn't it?"

"Sure is."

Just then a girl with short, dark hair came bouncing down the hallway. "Ex-*cuse* me," she called to Livvy and Suzy. "Is that *my* locker?"

Suzy's eyebrows shot up. Playfully, she jabbed Livvy. "Could this be Hot Pink?" she whispered.

Livvy groaned. "Oh great."

Suzy spun away to her own locker just as the girl came rushing up.

But Livvy stood her ground. "I'm assigned to this locker, too. We're locker partners for the year."

The girl stepped back, eyeing the upper shelf. "Looks like you've made yourself right at home."

"It was hard *not* to. I mean, I've never seen a carpeted locker before. You did a super job of decorating."

Hot Pink frowned, staring at the top section. "I was planning to use the upper shelf, but if you really want it . . ."

Livvy wasn't going to quarrel. New or not, she didn't need a hassle. "No, this is fine." She reached up and removed her books from the carpeted shelf. Squatting on the floor, she arranged them in her book bag.

Meanwhile, Hot Pink began to organize the bright shelf with her books. "It'll be tight quarters—with all my books and yours—but let's try to keep everything separate."

"Super."

Hot Pink whirled around. "What did you say?"

Livvy stood up. "I said, 'super.' "

And for the first time since Hot Pink had arrived, the two girls looked into each other's faces.

Unbelievable, thought Livvy. Her locker partner could've

passed for her pen pal's older sister. She recalled Jenna's school picture—the waist-length hair and the big smile.

Livvy continued to gawk. "Are you . . . could you be related to someone named Jenna Song? She lives near here."

Hot Pink burst out laughing. "Related?"

"It's just that you look so much like her." Livvy smiled, jostling her book bag. "Do you happen to know Jenna? Because she's my pen pal."

Hot Pink's eyes popped wide open. "You're . . . you've gotta be kidding."

"No, I've been writing to Jenna for several months now," Livvy said, wondering why the girl seemed so surprised.

"Are you an ice skater?" asked Hot Pink.

Livvy gulped. "How did you know?"

The girl gasped and covered her mouth. "Livvy? Olivia Hudson? What are *you* doing here?"

"I . . . I just moved here." She stared at her locker partner. "How do you know my name?"

"Because *I'm* your pen pal. I'm Jenna Song!"

Livvy was speechless. "You're Jenna? But your picture, your long hair—"

"The picture I sent you was last year's school picture. Besides, I had my hair cut short for school. It was a pain always putting my hair up for gymnastics and ballet."

All of a sudden they were hugging and giggling. "I wrote you a letter about moving," Livvy tried to explain. "Did you get it?"

"No, but that's because *we* were moving at the same time."

Livvy was going to burst. "I can't believe this! Why'd you move *here*?"

"Because my dad is the new pastor at the Korean church."

She grabbed her skate bag and closed the locker. "So that's why we're going to the same school!"

Jenna was still laughing as the two of them headed for the bus stop. "This is just too cool."

"I wonder how long it would've taken for us to actually meet."

Jenna smoothed her hair. "You mean if we hadn't been assigned the same locker?"

"It's super, isn't it?" Livvy meant it with all of her heart.

The girls waited for the bus together, still chattering about their first day of school.

"Where do you live?" asked Jenna.

"Main Street . . . in the tallest Victorian on the block." She didn't say the ugliest.

"My house is a couple of streets south of there. You'll have to visit sometime."

"Maybe we can have a sleep-over."

Jenna's grin reached from ear to ear. "Are you trying out for cheerleading?"

"Probably not."

"How come?"

She told Jenna about her plan to keep skating without a coach. "It'll be tough, but I'm not quitting."

"I don't blame you. You were right on track for the Olympics."

"Well, not quite *that* close."

Jenna turned to face her. "You're really good for your age. C'mon, Livvy, I don't know of many sixth-grade girls who reach novice level."

She couldn't deny it. But at the same time, she didn't want to think about what she'd given up back home.

"Why'd you and your dad move to Colorado anyhow?"

"Dad thought we needed a change of scenery," Livvy said. That was all she wanted to say. At least for now.

The bus pulled up to the curb just then. They waited for a group of kids to get on, then hurried up the steps and back as far as they could sit.

"So did you move because of your mom?" asked Jenna, her eyes full of concern.

Livvy felt horribly uncomfortable. She couldn't allow herself to talk about personal things. Not with Diane Larson sitting across the aisle, giving her the eyeball every other second. "Maybe we can talk later . . . in private. Okay?"

Jenna seemed to understand. "I'll call you tonight."

They exchanged phone numbers, and when the bus stopped in front of the little mall, Livvy slid out of the seat.

"Hey, where're you going?" Jenna called to her.

"To the ice rink." She couldn't help but notice Diane's hard frown. No way was *she* going to interfere with Livvy's skating plans.

Jenna leaped out of her seat. "Wait up, Livvy!"

Thrilled beyond belief, she waited for her hot-pink friend to catch up.

"You're just like me," Jenna declared as they walked

toward the mall entrance. "Completely obsessed."

"That's a good thing, I hope."

"Super good," Jenna added.

And they laughed at Jenna's use of Livvy's favorite word.

CHAPTER 9

August 31
Dear Grandma,

Today was the first day of school, and you'll never guess what happened. I met Jenna Song. She's my locker partner!

I thought moving to this town was going to be the worst thing that ever happened to me. And here I have a built-in best friend! She's in training . . . just like me. Only Jenna's a gymnast.

With Jenna to hang out with, I won't be constantly thinking about missing skating competitions. It's bad enough losing my coach, but now I have someone to talk to who understands my passion. And someone I'm hoping to attend ballet classes with!

Today after school she watched me skate at the mall rink. If I can talk Dad into it, Jen and I will be in the same ballet class.

Dad's working too hard, as always. This time it's the house. The place is going to be super nice when he's finished.

> *Write soon, okay?*
> *Love,*
> *Livvy*

She folded the letter and slid it into the middle drawer of her desk. Just in case she thought of something else to write. Like a P.S. or something.

After supper, the phone rang.

"I'll get it," Livvy called over the noise of the sander. She picked up the portable phone in the kitchen. "Hudson residence, Olivia speaking."

"Listen, and listen good," said a muffled voice. "Go back to where you came from."

"Excuse me?"

"I'm not saying this twice—you're not welcome here!"

Livvy didn't bother to wait for more. She felt weak in the legs and hung up.

"Who was on the line?" her dad called from the dining room. He'd stopped sanding partway through the phone call.

"Wrong number, I guess."

He went right back to making more racket. Livvy was relieved. She didn't want to tell him that someone at school was trying to frighten her. Probably Diane Larson. She was almost positive that's who had called, disguising her pitiful little voice.

The phone rang again.

Livvy's heart thumped. What should she say if it was the same person? She didn't want to lose her cool. The girl had no right to terrorize her!

Cautiously, she picked up the phone. "Hello?"

"Hi, it's Jenna."

Livvy was so relieved, she started laughing.

"What's so funny?"

Livvy explained. "I just got this bizarre call. It was so mysterious and . . . garbled, kinda. Like maybe the person didn't want me to know who was calling."

"Who do you think it was?" Jenna asked.

Livvy breathed deeply. "Might've been Diane Larson. She hates me, and I don't know why."

"Who's this girl, anyway?" asked Jenna.

"She shares the locker next to us . . . with Suzy Buchanan. The locker with all the gum wrappers."

"Oh yeah, I remember. Introduce me tomorrow, okay?" Jenna said.

"I'll give it a shot, but if Diane really wants me outta here, she won't stand still long enough to meet my best friend. Not if I'm the one doing the introductions."

"Are you sure Diane feels that way?"

"Positive."

"I wonder why."

"That's what I'm gonna find out," said Livvy.

They went on to talk about school and all their different subjects. Homeroom too.

"Middle school's so much better than grade school," Jenna said. "The biggest hassle is keeping all my teachers straight."

"I know what you mean. But maybe by the end of the week we'll know who's who." She hoped to steer their conversation away from personal things. "Isn't it cool, both of us being the new girls together?"

"Wouldn't have it any other way." Then Jenna excused herself. It sounded like she'd clamped her hand over the receiver.

Livvy could hear another voice in the background. She waited, wondering what was happening on the other end at the Song residence.

"Okay, I'm back," said Jenna. "My mom wants to know if you and your dad would like to come for supper this Saturday."

Livvy was speechless. She'd love to meet Jenna's parents, but she wasn't so sure if her dad would. He was mostly distant since Mom died. Especially around strangers.

"Tell your mom thanks, but I'll have to check with Dad. He's remodeling our house right now . . . the place is kind of trashed. Maybe when it's finished."

"Are you saying you might not come?"

She didn't want to offend her friend. Not for anything. "I'll have to ask."

"Okay. Just let me know."

Livvy felt suddenly anxious to get off the phone. "Sorry things are so messed up right now, Jen. I'll see you tomorrow."

"Everything okay?"

"Well, not exactly. But we'll talk later."

"Wait, Livvy..."

"I've got so much homework. Talk to you tomorrow. Bye." She hung up, feeling lousy. She'd shut out her dearest and best friend.

What *was* she thinking?

GO CHAPTER 10

Livvy awoke long before the clock radio sounded. She hadn't slept well. Her dreams had been disturbing.

The morning turned out lousy, too, including the discovery of curdled milk. She skipped eating cereal and had two pieces of toast and jelly and some applesauce instead.

At the rink, she missed nearly every jump. And when she tried her best camel spin, she toppled. Getting up, she worried that someone might've seen her pathetic performance. But when she glanced around, Livvy saw only an elderly man sitting on a bench near the rink. Tall and dressed for church or somewhere else special, the man looked like anyone's grandfather. No need to worry, she decided.

At about 6:45 a group of younger skaters showed up. Three girls and two boys. Livvy wondered where their instructor might be, but no adult arrived.

She pushed herself for an additional ten minutes, inching up her total skate time to a full half hour. Back home, there had been many days of two forty-minute sessions before school. Here in Podunk, she seemed to lose her focus after only one session.

Getting up the nerve, she skated over to one of the girls. "Where's your instructor?"

"She'll be here any minute now," said the girl. "Our coach likes us to warm up on our own sometimes."

Livvy hadn't seen this group of skaters before. "Do you skate here often?" she asked.

"Three times a week. On Saturdays we drive to Colorado Springs to the World Arena. It's fabulous."

"How far away?"

"Less than an hour."

"Thanks," Livvy said, feeling all jittery. If Colorado Springs was so close, maybe she could find herself a coach there. She'd have to get her dad to agree. *That* would be the biggest hurdle!

On the walk home, she thought of all the things she wanted to talk over with Dad. Ballet lessons, the Saturday night dinner invitation, and the possibility of having a new coach. And there was the problem of the spoiled milk, too.

Should she mention everything at once? Making sure the milk was fresh should be high on the list. Unless, of course, they could afford to have milk delivered to the house.

Livvy watched as the quaint little milk truck made its way down the street, stopping at one house, then the next.

"Things are falling apart here, Mom," she said into the air as she hurried home. "Sometimes I wonder if you can see how mixed up our lives are."

Then, just in case her mom *could* hear her complaining, she quickly added, "Please, Mom, don't worry . . . we'll make it somehow. I know we will."

For another whole block, she forced herself to walk quietly, without mumbling to her mother. It was hard, but she made it.

When the gray-and-white Victorian came into view, she quickened her pace. The skate bag bounced as she ran up the front steps and into the house. "Daddy, can we talk?" she called to him. Not waiting for an answer, she hurried into the kitchen. To the fridge.

There, on the top shelf, stood an unopened half gallon of fresh milk.

She heard footsteps and spun around. "Oh, Daddy, thanks for getting some more milk!" She ran to him, wrapping her arms around him.

"It's just milk, kiddo. No big deal."

But it *was* a big deal. One less thing on her mental list of concerns. She couldn't remember feeling so relieved.

They sat down together and poured cold milk over their frosted cereal. Livvy chattered all the while about school and meeting Jenna Song . . . and skating. "It's amazing what I found out today."

"What's that, honey?" Her dad was giving her his undivided attention for a change.

"Colorado Springs is only a short distance from here," she explained. "Maybe I could find a new skating coach there."

His face wrinkled into a frown. "What about transportation?"

"Maybe I could catch a ride with other skaters, or . . ." She wanted to say that maybe *he* could take her sometimes.

"Well, right now we don't have the money for a skating coach," he said. "Not here or in Colorado Springs."

"But . . . we had enough money before Mom died. Didn't we?"

Suddenly, he fell silent, and his eyes no longer made contact with hers.

She could've kicked herself. Right in the middle of a great conversation, she'd made a dumb mistake!

"I'm sorry, Dad. I didn't mean to say anything about Mom. I didn't—"

"Skating lessons are out of the question." His words were ice, and she dreaded the sound of them.

Now was not the time to bring up Jenna's supper invitation. Not ballet lessons, either. Livvy excused herself from the table and raced upstairs to shower and dress for school. She felt worse than ever. Actually, almost sick.

Her cockatiel tried to cheer her up, though. "Happy, happy Livvy," Coco chanted.

"Hush, bird." She slipped into her bathrobe.

His little white head cocked over to one side, his beady eyes blinking innocently. "Happy Livvy. Ha . . . ha . . . ha."

She couldn't stop the burst of air. It flew right past her lips. "I'm *not* even close to feeling happy, and you're one nosy parrot. That's no lie!"

"No lie . . . no lie."

Glancing at the clock, Livvy knew she'd have to rush to get ready. "I'll talk to *you* later."

"Livvy later . . . *caw*!"

In the shower, she scrubbed her body and shampooed her hair. All the while, she fretted over her slip-up at breakfast. *How long before I can talk about Mom in front of Dad?* she fumed.

She dressed faster than ever because she didn't want to be late for school. Not on the second day! Not on any day, come to think of it. Mrs. Smith had warned her homeroom about tardiness. Talk about strict.

Livvy did not want to write a 500-word essay! No matter what.

Jenna was waiting for her at their locker. "Well, can you come for dinner Saturday night?"

"I didn't ask my dad yet," Livvy confessed. "He was in a horrible mood this morning."

"Does he have to be in a good mood to decide about eating?"

She stared at Jenna, feeling uneasy. "Well, uh . . . it's kinda complicated." Livvy glanced around. "Can we talk at lunch?"

"Okay with me." Jenna turned to go. "See ya later."

Livvy pushed her skate bag back into the corner of the open locker. Then, standing up, she gazed down the crowded hallway. She felt terribly embarrassed and searched for Jenna, but her friend was nowhere in sight.

She stacked up her books in the lower section of the locker. And kept her math book and notebook out for first hour. "Thank goodness for homeroom," she mumbled to herself. At least she'd have time to calm down before her first class.

"Talking to yourself?"

Livvy turned to see Suzy lugging several books and her three-ring binder. She looked almost too small to be a seventh grader. "Oh, hi again."

Suzy squinted down the hall. "Hot Pink's kinda upset, looks like."

"How do you know?"

"I think she was praying . . . outside."

Livvy wasn't sure she'd heard right. "You sure?"

"Well, I saw her lips moving, and her eyes were definitely closed." Suzy twirled her combination lock, then pushed down on it.

Livvy leaned against her locker. "What's wrong with praying? It's a free country, isn't it?"

Suzy shrugged. "Just better watch out. She might try to get you on God's side, too."

Livvy wondered why Suzy was saying this. Jenna was one of the coolest girls around. And one of the best gymnasts on her team. Not to mention a really good friend.

"Lots of people pray," Livvy defended her friend. "Including me." She didn't feel like saying more. The truth was, it had been a very long time since she'd felt like praying.

Suzy taped another gum wrapper to the inside of her locker door. "Just don't expect Diane to go for any of that church stuff. From what Diane says, Jenna's dad is a pastor here in town somewhere."

"That's true, but how does Diane know so much about Jenna?"

A sly smile crossed Suzy's lips. "That girl knows everything about everyone. And don't say I didn't warn you." With that, the bell rang. Suzy darted into the stream of students.

Livvy remembered the weird phone call. "Wait!" she called after Suzy. But it was too late. Suzy had been gulped up by the homeroom rush.

Livvy dragged her feet to Room 123. She wished she'd stayed home in Chicago . . . with Grandma!

Lunch hour turned out far different than Livvy expected. No time to talk personally with Jenna. Not even five minutes' worth.

First off, Mrs. Newton came over and hung out at Livvy's table. Suzy showed up quickly. So did Jenna, wearing an enormous grin. Especially after Livvy informed her friend that Mrs. Newton was head of cheerleading.

Diane Larson didn't waste any time coming over, either. She squeezed in next to Suzy, her clear blue eyes merry with anticipation. "Who's gonna judge cheerleading tryouts?" she asked.

Mrs. Newton grinned. "You're lookin' at her."

Diane nodded. "Okay with me." She tapped her perfectly manicured fingernails on the table top.

"How many spots are open for just the seventh grade?" Suzy asked, glancing at Diane.

"Counting pompon girls, six." Mrs. Newton seemed excited. "We're getting new outfits this year for *all* the grades. The Cloth Mill is giving the school a discount on some expensive fabric."

Diane spoke up. "What're the patterns like?"

Suzy laughed. "Don't worry, the skirts are probably plenty cute, if that's what you're asking."

Mrs. Newton was nodding her head. "Pleated skirts, as always. But the tops are totally different this year."

Diane's face gleamed. "Like how?"

Moving her fingers, Mrs. Newton pretended to zip her lips. "My secret is sealed."

"Aw, please?" Diane begged.

Playfully, Jenna jabbed Livvy as they looked on.

"What're the school colors?" Livvy asked.

"Same as the Denver Broncos. Orange and navy blue." Mrs. Newton was obviously proud about that. "I'm a big fan of Alpine Lake Middle School," she informed Livvy and Jenna. "Betcha can't tell."

Livvy laughed. "Oh, we can tell, all right."

Mrs. Newton gave high fives to each girl before excusing herself.

"Isn't she something?" Livvy said when the woman had gone.

Jenna agreed. "Sure makes being the two new kids on the block a whole lot easier."

Diane's cheerful face turned to a scowl. "Don't go getting your hopes up about cheerleading."

Livvy shot back. "You haven't seen Jenna perform, have you? She'd make a fabulous cheerleader. She's one of the *best* gymnasts ever."

"I've heard," Diane replied, her eyes flashing with disdain. "Just don't hold your breath. Either of you!"

Livvy nudged Jenna's sleeve, trying to get her to leave the table.

"Don't bother to leave," Diane sneered. "We're outta here."

But Suzy wasn't going anywhere. "Speak for yourself, Larson," she hissed back. "I'm hanging with the new kids."

Definitely flustered, Diane batted her eyes. She shook her head and left in a huff.

Livvy and Jenna sat in the very back of the bus after school. In order to claim the coveted seats, they'd dashed out to the bus stop before any upperclassmen ever arrived.

"This is so cool," Jenna said, folding her arms and leaning back.

"We should do this more often," Livvy agreed as the bus pulled away from the curb. She looked ahead to Diane and several other girls in less-desirable seats halfway up, closer to the front.

She whispered to her friend about a couple of cute boys. "It's super being able to talk without Diane nosing around."

"Maybe, but I think she's having a rough time," Jenna said softly.

"Huh?"

"Diane needs us more than you think." Jenna's eyes were shining.

Livvy had no idea what she meant. "Are you for real?"

"Just watch her. She's wobbly."

Livvy observed Diane sitting with Suzy Buchanan. "Like unsure of herself?"

Jenna whispered, "No, just plain wobbly."

Livvy sighed. "You say the weirdest things."

"I do?" Jenna was laughing now. "Well, maybe there's a good reason."

"Like what?" Livvy was eager to know. Any info about Diane Larson would be helpful.

But Jenna only grinned.

"I'm waiting," said Livvy. And for the first time since she'd met Jenna face-to-face, her former pen pal seemed very mysterious.

"Waiting for what?"

"For you to tell me why you think Diane is more needy than nasty?"

"Sure, I'll tell you . . . *sometime*" came the secretive reply.

"Like when?"

"When you tell me why you moved out here."

So they both had a secret. Except Livvy was still trying to answer the "moving" question herself.

Grandma Hudson called right after supper and kept Dad on the phone for the longest time.

"Something wrong?" she asked as he hung up.

He was staring at her. "I guess it's time to call a family meeting."

"What's up with Grandma?"

He motioned her into the living room. "You may not be too thrilled about this." He sat at the end of the sofa. "I don't know how I feel about it, either."

Dad stopped talking for a moment.

"Is Grandma sick?" Livvy was still standing in the middle of the room.

"Better sit down, kiddo." He plumped the pillow next to him. "Your grandmother's worried about us."

"Well, somebody oughta be," Livvy mumbled.

Her father turned and looked at her, frowning. "Where on earth did *that* come from?"

She forced a puff of air past her lips. Now she'd have to explain herself for sure.

"I think it's time we level with each other." He began rolling his shirt sleeves up to the elbows. Like he was getting ready to tackle a major repair job.

She crossed her arms. "Are you actually going to hear me out?"

"Livvy . . . honey."

Her words sounded disrespectful, and she felt ashamed. "Can we *really* talk to each other, Daddy?" Her words came more softly.

Dad nodded, offering a winning smile. "Why don't you go first?"

So she did. She leaped right at the question and asked him why they'd come here. "I need to know," she said, her heart in her throat. "It was such a hard thing for me—leaving our real home behind."

His eyes shone suddenly with more than expectation.

When she saw the tears, Livvy wished she'd never brought up the question.

"Back home, it seemed that your mother was everywhere I looked," he began. "I couldn't think, sketch, or create without seeing her face."

A familiar ache stabbed her throat. She thought she might cry right there in front of him.

"You and I both needed a new place in the world, away from all the memories. We had to start over, Livvy."

"Maybe you needed to, but I needed to stay. I *wanted* to stay. Mom's buried back home. I can't ever go and sit beside her grave and talk . . . not in this town."

"But you do talk to her. . . ."

His words were unexpected. "How . . . how did you know?"

He put his arm around her and drew her close. "I've overheard some of your conversations, kiddo. Mostly in the early morning, when you think I'm out cold and don't hear you getting ready to head for the rink."

Sighing, she snuggled against her father. "I can't seem to let her go. I just can't. . . ."

"I'm not asking you to."

She could hear his heart beating against her ear.

"It's going to take a long time to get used to things the way they are," he said.

She wanted to say something about that but didn't think now was a good time to talk about skating. Or ballet.

They were silent long enough for Livvy to remember the reason why they were having this talk in the first place.

"What about Grandma Hudson?" she asked, sitting up. "Let's talk about her."

He leaned his elbows on his knees. "She wants to come for a visit."

"That's okay with me."

"Grandma wants to come here and try Alpine Lake on for size . . . maybe move in with us."

Livvy cringed. "You're kidding. Why?"

Dad turned and looked at her, his eyes searching hers. "She thinks you need a mother replacement."

Leaning back, Livvy covered her face with her hands. "She's my *grandmother*! No one can ever take Mom's place. She oughta know that!"

"Your grandmother means well."

"It'll never work, you'll see," she complained.

"I think we should give it a chance."

Livvy did *not* agree. But she wasn't going to let anything come between her and Dad. Not now, after their first heart-to-heart talk ever!

After skating the next morning, Livvy came home to find her Dad up and dressed. "We've been invited for supper," she said as casually as possible. Hoping . . . hoping.

"Where to?" He was stirring up some eggs and milk at the counter. Making a mess.

"Jenna Song's mom invited us to their house Saturday night. Wanna go?"

He shrugged a little. "If you'd like to . . . sure."

"You mean it?" She hugged him, then cleaned up the spills around the mixing bowl. "This is incredible!"

"Having dinner with your friends might help us fit in better around here."

She felt light enough to float. "I'll tell Jenna first thing." Scurrying off to clean up and put on fresh clothes, Livvy could hardly wait to see her friend's expression. "This is soo super!" she squealed to herself, taking the steps two at a time.

Upstairs, Coco got all excited, too. He started squawking back at her.

"Calm down, fella," she cooed, tapping his cage gently. "Nothing for *you* to get wound up about."

As she spun around the room, her feet could hardly keep from dancing. Maybe her dad was coming out of his hermit's shell. Maybe things were going to change.

Flying around the spacious room, she felt dizzy and stopped in front of her calendar. The featured world-champion ice skaters seemed to be spinning, too. Both guys and girls.

She reached up and flipped the pages back past August and July, to June tenth. The saddest day of her life, forever marked with a sad face.

Life as she'd known it had stopped on that date. For Dad, too. She knew that no matter how many Saturday suppers they attended, the pain of losing Mom was never going to disappear.

Jenna was sporting an orange T-shirt and navy blue pants when she boarded the bus that morning. Some of the boys cheered, and Livvy giggled about it.

"Back here!" she waved, calling to her friend.

"Why'd the boys carry on like that?" Jenna whispered to her as she settled into the seat.

"Because you're cute, silly."

Jenna laughed and fluffed her short hair. "It's probably the orange and blue colors. I heard it was school spirit day."

"No one said anything in homeroom yesterday." She looked down at her own faded blue jeans and white T-shirt. "Are you sure?"

"Well, Diane Larson called me last night. That's how I heard."

"Sounds like a trick to me."

"Well, if it is, I fell for it." Jenna straightened her iridescent orange shirt. "But, oh well . . ."

"How can you just do that?" Livvy stared at her.

"Do what?"

"You know, pretend like it's nothing."

Jenna piled her book bag on her lap. "It's not easy getting along with someone like Diane. But I have this feeling about her. Like I told you, I think she needs a true friend."

It was the way Jenna said *true* that made her wonder. Something about it reminded her of Grandma Hudson's approach to things. Her dad's mother had always been one to forgive and forget quickly.

"Hey, I have some good news," Livvy said. "We're coming to your house on Saturday. If we're still invited."

"You sure are!" Jenna squeezed her hand. "This is so cool!"

"I didn't know what Dad would decide. He's been hiding away from the world—like a hermit—since Mom died."

Jenna nodded. "I don't blame him. Do you?"

The comment took her breath away. Her friend had a way of firing off unexpected questions. "Well, I think I understand why he'd wanna stay away from people. It's been just a little over two months since we lost Mom."

"Maybe that's why your dad picked Alpine Lake. It's far away from the past, isn't it?"

Livvy felt like she was being quizzed. "Dad and I had a long talk last night. Bottom line: He says we needed to get away from our old house back in Illinois."

"Because it reminded him of your mother?"

Livvy nodded thoughtfully.

The bus made another stop. Suzy and Diane came on board, laughing and talking to each other. Livvy was thankful that they found seats close to the front.

They waited for the traffic light to turn, then the bus jerked forward. All the while, Livvy stared at the back of Diane's head. *Is she the mystery caller?*

Livvy turned and looked out the window, watching the old clapboard houses and the cars whiz by. She longed for the old days as tears blurred her vision.

"I've been praying for you, Livvy," her friend said.

Livvy fought the lump in her throat, still gazing out the window. "Thanks," she managed to say.

"Ever since you wrote me about your mom's illness," Jenna added.

Jenna's remark touched her heart. And Livvy was ashamed for not praying much herself.

They rode along in silence. Halfway to school, Jenna pulled something out of her pants pocket. "Before I forget . . . your letter finally came."

Livvy studied the double postmark. "Looks like it got forwarded to your new address."

"You called this town Podunk, USA, in your letter, re-member?" Jenna was grinning about it. "But you know what? I think I like that name almost better than Alpine Lake."

Now *both* of them were gawking out the bus window. Livvy noticed there were fewer trees here than back home. Mostly tall Ponderosa pines. Rugged and irregular, they were different from the trees in Chicago. Everything was different here.

"Podunk's pretty tiny, isn't it?" Jenna said, snickering again. "But you should've seen the place where we used to live. My dad called it a 'one-horse town.' And I'm not kidding."

"One horse or one mall?" asked Livvy.

"Oh, we had a little mall, all right," said Jenna. "But nothing to brag about."

"Like Podunk?" Livvy said.

"Yep," answered Jenna, laughing.

Livvy couldn't help but laugh, too.

Livvy stopped in to see Mrs. Newton at the Cloth Mill after school.

The woman seemed pleased to see her. "How would you like a sneak preview of the new cheerleader outfits?" she asked.

"I thought they were top secret."

"Well, I can trust *you*, can't I?" The woman's bangles and bracelets jingle-jangled as she motioned Livvy over to a wall cupboard. She reached up to turn the knob but paused in midair. "Here we are." Out came yards and yards of soft navy blue fabric and the top-secret pattern.

Livvy was still surprised that Mrs. Newton was showing her the pattern. "Who will sew the outfits?" she asked.

"Oh, you'd be surprised at the moms who'll volunteer."

Livvy nodded slowly, thinking of the many sewing projects she and her mom had shared together over the years.

"Oh, my dear, have I got no heart?" Mrs. Newton was

saying. "I've gone and lost my head, it seems." And she asked Livvy to please forgive her. "Such an unthinking person I must be."

"No, not at all," Livvy insisted. Here was the perfect time to tell the woman how very kind she had been. Right from the start. "It's super nice to have someone like you as a friend."

"Why, thank you, Livvy. I'm proud to call you my friend, too." There was a glint in her expressive eyes. "I've been watching you skate," she said, her voice growing even more sweet. "During my break, I've seen you working out all by yourself."

"You have?"

"Oh yes, and you're very good." Mrs. Newton told her how she liked to stop off and have a cup of coffee at the Oo-La-La Café. "Right across from the rink, that's where I sip and watch," the woman said, looking mighty pleased with herself.

Livvy grinned, delighted with the compliment. "Well, thank you. I'm not used to people watching me practice anymore." She hesitated at first, then found herself pouring out her grief. She talked mostly of her father's lack of interest. "I don't think Daddy understands how badly I want to go to the Olympics someday."

Mrs. Newton patted her hand. "Stick to your dreams, Livvy. You must never give up on yourself." She chuckled a little. "My goodness, not as talented as you are."

She was almost afraid the woman would ask if she was going to try out for cheerleading. But they talked about everything *but* that. And Livvy was relieved.

She hated to say good-bye. But it was time to hit the ice. Today her goal was to push for a forty-minute session. Do or die!

Mrs. Newton's words of encouragement echoed in her brain, and she grinned to herself. Near the rink, she found a half-occupied bench and began to remove her tennis shoes.

The same grandfatherly man sat at the opposite end, a rolled-up newspaper in his hand. Instead of reading, he was watching several skaters as they practiced their technique.

"Excuse me, do you happen to have the time?" she asked, leaning over.

He glanced at his watch, then grinned at her. "Skate time or otherwise?"

"Otherwise, please." She didn't give his clever comment a second thought.

Promptly, he added, "It's nearly three-thirty."

"Thank you."

"You're very welcome, young lady." He unfolded his paper and shook it out. "Please, don't mind me. You go on and have fun skating."

She pulled on her white skates and laced up. Livvy could hardly wait to warm up. Skating was like flying—or better. The slick surface beneath her blades made her feel absolutely free. Like escaping from every imaginable problem and pain of her life.

Today she pretended to skate for a packed crowd, filled with hundreds of cheering fans. Soaring across the rink, she practiced some of her best fancy footwork.

Then, when she was ready, she posed at center ice. Waiting as if for the musical cue, she began her short program—the one from her last regional event. She could still hear the music in her head, the dazzling score from *Anastasia*.

She didn't have to hum the phrases to remember where her jumps and spins fit in. The thrilling strains filled her, and the performance was smooth and elegant. One of the best practices she'd had since coming to Podunk town.

"I skated my best, Mom," she whispered as she began cooling down. "I did it."

In her imagination, the fans were standing, throwing teddy bears onto the ice. Thunderous applause! She could almost see the young skaters darting here and there as they picked up bouquets of flowers. *Her* flowers! Just the way she hoped it would be someday at the Olympics.

Someday, if she ever found another coach. If she ever got back every ounce of her confidence. . . .

After supper, Livvy sprawled on the couch. The living room windows yawned wide and still the house was warm. Much too hot to do homework or anything else.

Livvy decided to relax in front of the TV for a while. After a few boring scenes, she gave in to the scratchy feeling beneath her eyelids. She closed her eyes—just to rest a bit— and she was in dreamland. Lake Placid, New York, where some of the best skaters in the world train. . . .

In her dream, she heard the musical introduction for her free-skate program. The soul-stirring strains from the over-ture-fantasy *Romeo and Juliet* by Tchaikovsky started her four-minute routine. Her flowing green costume made her feel like an ice princess with its Austrian crystals sewed on the bodice, sleeves, and hem. They sparkled like diamonds under the arena lights, and she skated her heart out for the enthusiastic crowd.

Just as she was awaiting the judges' marks, the phone

rang and woke her. The exciting dream was shattered.

She figured her dad had picked up the phone because she heard his voice in the kitchen. *Probably Grandma again*, she thought. Nestling back into the sofa pillows, she hoped she might recapture the glorious images.

"Livvy, are you awake? Someone wants to talk to you."

Groaning, she pulled herself up off the couch. "I'm coming."

Still tired from skating, she staggered through the dining room and into the kitchen. She sat down and picked up the phone. "Hello?"

"Why are you still here in Alpine Lake?" came the haunting, muddled voice.

Not frightened, Livvy confronted the caller. "Who *are* you?"

"I'm telling you, for your own good—go back home. You don't belong here!"

She wished her dad had hung around so she wasn't alone with this phone weirdo. Instead of freaking out, though, she decided to stand her ground. *"This* town is my home now."

"Not for long, Miss Livvy."

Something about the way the voice was starting to lose its raspy sound made her think of Diane Larson. Again!

"Who's *Miss* Livvy? I don't know anyone by that name." She baited the caller, hoping to trick the person into speaking more clearly.

"I know your name! It's Livvy, the loser."

With each word, the voice sounded more like Diane. So Livvy decided to keep her talking for as long as possible.

"You've gotta be mistaken, whoever you are. Because I'm

a winner. I *know* I am . . . and I'm going to stay right here in Alpine Lake. You can forget about calling me anymore." She was surprised at how confident she sounded. Even to herself!

"Listen, girl, I'm not kidding. Leave town or . . . or . . ."

There was sudden silence.

"Or what? You just might get beat out at cheerleading tryouts? Is that what you're afraid of, Diane?"

A little gasp came through the phone. Then *click*—the caller hung up.

Livvy immediately dialed her friend. She had to tell Jenna the news.

Jenna answered on the first ring. "Hello?"

"Hi, it's Livvy, and guess what? I'm pretty sure Diane's the one who called me the other night, trying to scare me out of town."

"Are you sure?"

Livvy revealed every detail of tonight's phone call. Even the awkward silence. "It was like she wanted to threaten me, but she couldn't do it."

"Wow . . . I was right" came the mysterious reply.

"About what?"

"About Diane. She's not a bad kid, she's just dying for attention."

"Well, that's a bizarre way of getting it!"

"I feel sorry for Diane," Jenna said softly.

This was the last thing Livvy wanted to hear. "The girl's a troublemaker," she said. "You know it, and so do I."

"I know you probably won't understand this, but I think

we oughta invite Diane to do something with us . . . soon. The *three* of us."

"You wouldn't say that if you'd heard Diane's hateful voice tonight on the phone," Livvy retorted. "So count me out!"

"Well, if you're sure," Jenna replied. "But I'd like to hang out with her a little. Maybe eat lunch with her tomorrow. Okay with you?"

Livvy despised the idea. She couldn't imagine sharing Jenna with anyone, let alone a hateful girl like Diane Larson!

CHAPTER 15

The group of five skaters was working on circular skat-ing steps when Livvy arrived the next morning. Their coach was a petite young woman with blond hair pulled back in a sleek French braid.

On the sidelines, the smartly dressed gentleman sat on the same bench as yesterday. She guessed he was a drifter, though she wondered about his nice clothes. Maybe he was just someone who needed a place to sit and rest. Or maybe he was a lonely old man who enjoyed watching the skaters.

The mall was the ideal shelter from the wind and rain outside. Free from the early fall drizzle that Livvy had slopped through to get here.

Stealing another glance at the man, she tightened her skates. He seemed more interested in his surroundings than his newspaper at the moment.

Mall walkers were out in full force. Probably because of the weather. She wished that someday she could get her dad to come here and exercise with the rest of the town. And while her dad walked, she could skate. A super setup. If she could just coax him to get up early . . . and *other* important things. Like agreeing to pay for skating and ballet lessons.

She stood up and did a few back-stretching exercises. When she caught the man looking her way, she waved. "Hello again. How are you today?"

"Just dandy," he answered with a wrinkled smile. A pad of paper lay on the bench beside him. Probably checking the newspaper ads for odd jobs.

She stretched some more and did twenty-five jumping jacks, swinging her arms back and forth, before ever taking to the ice. When she'd run through her warm-ups, Livvy did several easy jumps—two double flips and three double toe loops—one after the other as she worked her way across the rink.

Sharing the ice with the other less-experienced skaters and their young coach, Livvy was careful to keep a safe distance. She practiced a combination spin, changing her feet and her position while keeping her speed. She practiced it again and again, at least fifteen times. Next, she circled the ice, shaking the kinks out of her legs.

But as hard as she tried to focus, Livvy's thoughts kept drifting back to last night's phone conversation. The oddest thing was that Jenna insisted on being kind to Diane. Her plan was absurd. It bugged Livvy. Her best friend wanted to hang out with the meanest girl in town!

Why?

The idea of having to overlook Diane's horrible, near-threatening remarks—the way Jenna had—frustrated Livvy. Made her *furious*!

Jenna should be taking Livvy's side against Diane. Wasn't that how best friends were supposed to treat each other?

She dreaded going to school. Even thought of skipping today, just this once. She could stay here at the rink and practice off and on all day long.

It was a super idea while it lasted. But she knew her father would be horrified. And knowing her homeroom teacher, Mrs. Smith would probably slap an enormous essay on top of all of Livvy's other homework!

No, it wouldn't be worth it. She'd have to face Jenna and deal with things as they were. As for Diane Larson, well . . . she couldn't even begin to think about *her*!

Gritting her teeth, Livvy was determined to turn her angry energy into something positive. She took a deep breath and, without music, skated through her entire short program.

She was careful to make every jump, including the triple toe loop. Then came the double Salchow. There were several preparations for the jump, and up until two days ago, Livvy worried that she wasn't ready. But she did her clockwise back crossovers and moved onto her takeoff leg.

Into the air she flew, landing gracefully on the back outside edge of her skate blade—only a quarter-inch wide.

"Yes!" she shouted, arms high overhead. Her constant, everyday practice—on her own—had paid off.

The other skaters were clapping. So was their coach.

Livvy happened to look above the rink, to the bench beneath the tree. There was the old man, standing and clapping, too.

Bowing, she imagined that he was a well-known European judge at an international competition. She thought he wore a smile just for her, so she offered a second bow. Just for him.

"Hey, you're *good*!" one of the girls said.

"Thanks," Livvy said, catching her breath.

Soon, she was surrounded by all five of the skaters. Their coach, too. "Do you train around here?" the coach asked, her blue eyes dancing.

Livvy explained that she'd come from Illinois. "My name is Olivia Hudson. But everyone calls me Livvy."

"Nice to meet you, Livvy. I'm Natalie Johnston. Have you found a new coach yet?"

"Not yet." She felt uncomfortable explaining why.

"Well, if I were qualified to teach advanced skaters, I'd certainly love to work with you."

"Thanks," Livvy replied.

They talked awhile longer, and Livvy was surprised to learn that Natalie was also a ballet instructor. "I have a large practice studio in my house," Natalie explained. "On Main Street."

"That's my street, too," Livvy said. "320 Main."

Natalie raised her eyebrows. "So you must be the folks who bought the gray Victorian." She could easily have said, "The run-down piece of junk in the middle of the block," but Natalie was kind.

"It was my dad's idea to fix up the house. He's an artist."

Natalie grinned. "So . . . you're my neighbor. Just two houses down."

Livvy was delighted. She couldn't wait to tell her dad the news. She could attend ballet classes on weekends and never have to ask for a ride.

Suddenly, she was thirsty and had forgotten to bring her sports bottle along. Slipping the rubber protectors over her blades, she headed for the water fountain near the rest rooms.

Coming back, she stopped near the wooden bench to talk to the old man. Before she could speak, he stood up to greet her.

"My compliments to you, missy. You're in excellent form today."

"Thank you, uh, Mr. . . . sir." She noticed the twinkle in his gray-blue eyes, wondering if it was polite to ask his name.

"Please, excuse my bad manners," he said, extending his hand. "Allow me to introduce myself. My name is Odell Sterling. Most folks call me Sterling. It's shorter, you see. People are in a hurry these days."

She shook his hand politely. "I'll call you *Mister* Sterling, then, if that's all right."

He nodded. "And I suppose your name is Her Grace, for you are certainly light-footed and graceful on the ice."

"Thank you." She laughed a little. "That's one compliment I've never received." She went on to tell him her name but didn't bother with her *real* nickname. Because she secretly liked Her Grace better.

He picked up his pen and note pad. For a moment, he

studied something on the paper. "I watched your setup for each of your jumps, Olivia," he said at last.

"You did?" She felt self-conscious.

"Perhaps you might achieve more control by gaining increased speed . . . before you go into your backward jumps."

Elena had drummed the same thing into her, over and over. And she told him so. "My coach back home was always reminding me of that."

She observed the man, this Mr. Sterling. He had to be way past fifty years old, maybe closer to sixty. She couldn't tell for sure. His hair was mostly brown, very little gray. But it was the ruddy face, populated by wrinkles, that made her guess he was older than even Grandma Hudson.

"How do you know so much about skating?" she asked, sitting on the edge of the bench.

He waved his hand as if batting a fly. "Oh, I suppose I've watched my share of skating events, like most anybody," he replied. "A person can pick up an awful lot from those slick-talking announcers, you know."

She told him she'd enjoyed watching televised sports events, too, as a young girl. "So it sounds like we have something in common," she said, getting up.

"You're the girl with talent," he agreed. "And I just appreciate what I see."

"Do you live in Podunk . . . er, Alpine Lake?" she asked.

He'd caught what she'd said. Chortling, he repeated it. "Podunk's quieter than most places I've lived. But I like it here . . . in Podunk." There was a mischievous look in his eyes.

"I guess I oughta say Alpine Lake."

"Aw, go on and call it whatever you like," he said, leaning back against the bench. "A place is only as good as its nickname."

"Where else have you lived?"

"New York . . . that's my home state."

"Ever go to Lake Placid?" she asked.

"All the time." A fleeting look of joy glimmered in his eyes. "The best years of my life."

She was more curious than ever. "Did you get to meet any of the world's best skaters?"

"Oh, a few." But he stood up with a grunt, as if he was ready to leave.

"Well, I guess we could talk all day. Sorry to keep you, Mr. Sterling."

He motioned toward the rink. "You have some more skating to do before school, Her Grace."

"I sure do!" She beamed back at him, wondering if he'd be here waiting after school.

He called his "good-byes," and she did the same.

Then she bent down to tighten the laces on her right skate. That's when she noticed the note pad. He must've dropped it. Reaching under the bench, she retrieved it. She saw his name written on the outside but didn't allow herself to peek inside.

When she looked up, she saw the man walking toward the food court. She would've run after him but couldn't risk ruining her best skates.

So she slipped the note pad into her bag and decided to return it the next time she saw him. Probably this afternoon.

Preparing to leave the rink and head for home, she thought about the old man's nickname for her. "Her Grace," she said aloud.

She twirled around, her skate bag flying as she made her way to the mall entrance. All the way home she thought about Odell Sterling, wondering why his name sounded so familiar.

CHAPTER 16

Livvy managed to avoid seeing Jenna before school. She even waited till her locker partner was finished getting her books and things out before heading down the hall.

When both Jenna and Diane were safely heading off to homeroom, Livvy dashed out from behind one of the class-room doors.

Just then the first bell rang.

She had to hurry—Mrs. Smith would be waiting. In more ways than one!

Her fingers fumbled the combination lock, but she managed to open the locker and stash away her skate bag. She grabbed up her math and English books and slammed the door shut.

"Whoa, are you in a rush or what?" Suzy asked, running toward her.

"Run for your life."

"What's the hurry? We're having an assembly first thing."

"I still can't be late for homeroom . . . bye!" Livvy ran to Room 123.

The tardy bell rang. Louder than usual.

She zipped past the doorway. And Mrs. Smith glanced up from her desk just as Livvy slid into her seat. She felt like a baseball player stealing home.

"Miss Hudson" came the disappointing words.

She knew to slump in her seat would be a big mistake. So she sat as straight and tall as possible. "Yes, Mrs. Smith."

"You're tardy."

"I'm sorry, it won't happen again."

Livvy felt her muscles tense up. Not a good thing for a skater on her way to fame and glory. A terrible thing, actually.

Here it comes. She braced herself for the worst possible writing assignment in all of Podunk.

"Miss Hudson, you will write . . ." The teacher paused.

Livvy realized she was holding her breath. When she inhaled, she began to blink her eyes. Fast.

"Are you all right?" Mrs. Smith asked.

"I . . . I think so."

"Very well. I'll expect to see your written assignment on my desk first thing—well before the last bell—tomorrow. Write a 300-word letter, Olivia. Write it to a student here at Alpine Lake Middle School."

A letter?

She was super at letters. She'd write one to her old pen pal. This was too good to be true!

She pulled out some paper to take notes.

"In the letter, I want you to describe the meaning of tardy. Why it's important to be on time for school . . . and for life."

Livvy began to take notes. While Mrs. Smith was still talking, Livvy jotted down the guidelines for the assignment.

"Excuse me, Olivia."

She looked up. "Yes?"

"Please, you must *never* write when I'm talking."

Livvy gasped.

The pet peeve!

How could she have forgotten?

Instantly, she put her pen down. But she knew by the teacher's stern face she'd committed an unforgivable flub.

"Make that two letters, to two different students. One, explaining the importance of being prompt. The second, describing the significance of following rules in general."

Mrs. Smith was ticked off. No question.

Livvy didn't know whether to apologize or to keep her mouth shut. In the end, she wished she'd stayed at the rink. But who knows what sort of letter *that* misdeed would have required.

She was in hot water, and she knew it. Now . . . how to keep from drowning! With the homework assignments of the day yet to be given, and the after-school practice session at the rink, Livvy wondered how she would pull off two acceptable letters. And to students!

Mrs. Smith continued. "I expect to receive these written

assignments directly. In other words, bring your letters to me."

If she hadn't been so angry at Jenna, Livvy might've weathered the blow. But lunch period turned out to be another disaster. "One after another," she said to herself, gazing across the cafeteria.

She could see Jenna and Diane sitting together, laughing and talking. And she could hardly stand to watch. Too many glances toward her best friend and her worst enemy wouldn't do. So she made herself look only at her brown lunch bag.

"What're you doing way over here?" Suzy asked, sneaking up.

"None of your business," she snapped. "Go sit with your locker partner."

"If you say so." Suzy must've spotted where Diane was sitting. "Okay, I see her. Bye!"

Once again, Livvy was alone.

She dug around in her book bag and found the small note pad belonging to Odell Sterling. Fighting nosiness, she tried to imagine what might be written inside. She had no right to read someone's private writings. So she placed it on the table, while she had several more bites of her chicken and tomato sandwich.

Several times throughout her lunch, she caught herself staring at Mr. Sterling's note pad. *What was he writing while*

I skated? she wondered. *Why was an old man taking notes at the rink?*

At last, her curiosity got the best of her. She opened the flap and saw line after line of scribble. Scanning the first page, she tried to read the words.

When she'd finished, she flipped to the next page. Soon she'd read every word.

"He knows skating," she whispered. "Who *is* Odell Sterling?"

Wanting to take good care of the old man's tiny notebook, she slipped it back into her book bag for safekeeping.

Then, to save time, she began working on her assigned letters for Mrs. Smith. While she nibbled on pretzel sticks, she started writing the one on the tardy theme.

Dear Jenna,

This is a required letter. It's to you from me, and I hope you'll understand what the word "tardy" means by the end of it.

I was a few seconds behind the bell for homeroom this morning. It's not the first time I've ever been late, though. Once, when I was in fourth grade, I forgot to set my alarm and missed my skating session. It messed things up big time for me.

You know why? Because I didn't get to skate in the local competition. I should have learned my lesson back then.

She stopped writing. Someone was staring at her. Livvy was sure of it.

Slowly, she looked up. There stood Diane.

The spiteful girl glanced at the chair across from her. "Mind if I sit down?"

Livvy tried to cover the letter, but she folded it instead and pushed it down into her sock.

"Look, I've been a jerk," Diane said, her clear eyes holding their gaze.

Livvy nearly choked. "Excuse me?"

"Your best friend just filled me in and—"

"*Jenna* talked to you about me?"

Diane nodded her head up and down. "I decided the day you enrolled for school that I didn't like you. I heard you were a star skater or something."

"A novice."

"Well, that's supposed to be really good . . . for a sixth grader, anyway."

Livvy didn't know whether to say "thanks" or "get lost."

But Diane wasn't finished. "I didn't want to get squeezed out of my chance at cheerleading. Or anything else around here. It's a small school and . . . and I was jealous of you."

"What did Jenna say about me?" Livvy asked.

"Just that you're the coolest friend ever. And that your mother died last summer." Diane's eyes blinked awkwardly. "I can't imagine not having my mom around . . . and I can't think of going off somewhere new to live, where kids like me act like morons." She stopped to find a tissue in her pocket. "What I'm trying to say is, I'm sorry, Livvy. I never should've called you on the phone like that. It was a cruel thing to do."

Livvy shook her head. "You didn't scare me—not really. I was mostly just mad."

"So . . . can we be friends?" Diane's eyes were pleading.

Out of the corner of her eye, Livvy spotted Jenna. She was smiling that winning smile of hers. "Friends? Sure."

After Diane left, Jenna wandered over. "You shouldn't be eating alone over here. You know better than that, girl."

"Yeah, so?"

"I see Diane talked to you." Jenna pulled her hair back, then let it float free.

"Very funny . . . you set it all up." She gathered up her trash. "You're a real peacemaker, aren't you?"

"That's what friends are for."

Livvy took a long drink of her pop while Jenna picked at her pretzel sticks. She told her about being tardy for homeroom. "Now I have to write a long letter to someone as an assignment. I picked you, but you'll never read it."

"That's what *you* think!"

Livvy took another sip of soda and felt something tickling her leg. "Why you!"

Jenna had reached down and pulled the letter out of Livvy's sock.

"Give that back!"

"No way." Jenna pretended to scan the letter, holding it high, out of Livvy's reach.

Mrs. Smith strolled by just then.

Livvy didn't want to chance another humiliating scene with her homeroom teacher. "Oh, so what. Go ahead and read it," she said, giving up.

Surprisingly, Jenna returned the letter, eyes smiling. "I know what tardy means, silly. I wasn't *too late* with Diane, was I?"

"Somehow, you knew it was time."

Jenna glanced up. "It helps to talk things over with Someone who knows all things."

"I figured you'd say that."

"He's never too late, Livvy."

"I know."

The table at Jenna's house was lit with several tall candles in a floral centerpiece. Jenna's mother insisted on serving each person. And Livvy was amazed at the way the Saturday night supper was presented. The dishes were ornate with Oriental themes and swirling, colorful designs.

"It's wonderful to finally meet our Jenna's pen pal"— Reverend Song smiled at Livvy—"and her father." Then he turned to engage Livvy's dad in small talk.

Livvy worried that her father might clam up and make things awkward all evening. She honestly didn't know what to expect. As quiet and withdrawn as he was, Livvy could only hope that her dad would try to fit in. At least for this one evening.

"I understand you are the new pastor in town," her dad remarked as they sat at the elegant table.

Reverend Song nodded, his eyes squinting a smile. "Yes, and what a delight to know that by moving here, our daughters will be able to become better acquainted."

Livvy grinned at Jenna, sitting next to her. "I think our dads are getting along just fine," she whispered.

Jenna nodded. "They ought to . . . they have *us* in common."

When the hot tea was poured in each tiny cup, Mrs. Song sat down. Her husband bowed his head and began to bless the food. "Thank you, Father in heaven, for this evening together with new friends. I ask a special blessing on Livvy and her father as they put down roots in this small community. And I pray that you will lead and direct them. May they experience your divine love and wisdom." He went on to thank the Lord for the food and the hands that prepared it.

All the while, Livvy clasped her own hands in her lap, paying close attention to this kind and gracious man's prayer.

After a full-course Korean dinner, Jenna took Livvy upstairs to her room. They hung out together, laughing and talking, while Livvy's dad chatted with Jenna's parents in the living room.

Later, when she was alone in her own room, Livvy knelt beside her bed. "Dear Lord, I'm sorry about ignoring you for so long. I guess you know how angry I've been."

She sighed. "It wasn't easy losing Mom, especially when I wish you would've done something to stop it. But that doesn't mean I don't still have faith in you . . . with all of my heart. Please help Dad come to believe in you soon. Let him know your love and that you didn't let Mom die to punish him—just because he isn't a Christian yet."

At the end of her prayer, Livvy thanked God for bringing her to Alpine Lake, "even if it's the Podunkiest town on earth. Amen."

Two days later, Grandma Hudson arrived. Livvy rode along with her dad to the Colorado Springs airport.

"There's my honeybunch," Grandma said, squeezing Livvy's cheek.

"Hi, Grandma. Welcome to Colorado." Livvy stepped forward as passengers walked past her.

Her dad kissed his mother, offering to carry the overnight case. "The altitude's much higher here than Illinois," he warned, "so you may have to take things slow and easy."

"Oh, I'll adjust in no time," Grandma said.

Livvy spoke up. "If you drink lots of water, it helps take away altitude sickness."

"But some folks never have any trouble," Dad said, hugging Grandma once again. "We're going to have a wonderful time together."

"How long can you stay?" Livvy asked. She was hoping for a four- or five-day response . . . maybe even a week. But not more than that.

Grandma raised her eyebrows and offered a broad smile. "Well, I'll just have to see about that. Looks to me like you could use a good dose of mothering, Olivia Kay. Are you eating three good meals a day?"

Livvy nodded reluctantly. She was eating just fine—and cooking for her dad, too!

All the way up the long concourse to the main terminal, she wondered what Grandma meant about "a good dose of mothering." The idea that her father's mother had come to take over the household worried Livvy. She noticed that her grandmother had packed very light. Maybe things would be super fine after all.

Livvy could only hope so.

CHAPTER 18

One week later, Livvy and Jenna were eating ice cream at the Oo-La-La Café. They'd chosen a table outside on the patio section of the tiny mall restaurant. The breezes were warm and gentle.

"September in the mountains isn't so bad," Livvy said.

"Sounds like Podunk is growing on you," said her friend.

"Oh, maybe . . ." Livvy's ice cream was melting fast. Licking it kept her from having to say more.

"My mom signed me up for ballet classes," Jenna said out of the blue.

"With Natalie Johnston?"

Jenna's mouth dropped open. "How'd you know?"

Livvy told her about meeting Natalie and her students at the ice rink. "I see her working with her skaters several times a week. She seems really nice."

"My mom thought so, too. She interviewed her yesterday and toured her dance studio. I can't wait."

Livvy's heart sank. She wished *she* could say she was signing up. One thing at a time, her mother had always said.

"It'll be tough juggling gymnastics and ballet," Jenna told her. "But I have my goals. And I decided not to try out for cheerleading."

"Me neither."

Jenna spooned up her chocolate ice cream. "Gotta keep focused."

"Speaking of that, I have a date with an ice rink," Livvy said, grabbing a napkin out of the holder. She wiped up the melted mess off the table before excusing herself.

"I'll come by later," Jenna said. "We can walk to my house afterward."

"Okay. See ya." Livvy hurried the few yards through the café to the mall.

She wasn't too surprised to see Mr. Sterling again. He was wearing blue dress pants and a white long-sleeved shirt. He looked dashing, almost younger than his years. As usual, he sat on his favorite bench.

Someone else was there, too. Mrs. Newton, all decked out in bangles and bows.

"Ready for the show?" she asked, looking at both of them.

"Skate away," said Mrs. Newton. "That's why we're here."

Mr. Sterling inched up his shirt sleeve, studying his wrist watch. "Her Grace is right on time." He chuckled and settled back against the bench.

"I've learned my lesson about being late!" Livvy remembered the strange assignment she'd written for her homeroom teacher.

Taking her time, she pulled on her skates. She'd learned so much already right here at this mall rink. By herself. Yet, to be honest about it, she knew that most of her practice methods had come straight from Elena. All those years with such a super coach . . .

Livvy had come to accept the fact that she could only go so far on her own. Somehow, it seemed all right. Because today she would not daydream about performing for a huge audience. Today she would skate her heart out for two wonderful people. Two of her biggest fans.

Above all, she would enjoy her skate session for herself. *I'll just have fun*, she promised.

She took the ice with more energy and dash than she'd ever known. At least since her arrival here.

First one spin, then another. Fancy footwork across the width of the rink. Next, Livvy flew into the air, smiling as she practiced her jumps. She was having such a good time.

When forty minutes had come and gone, she could hardly believe it! And she wouldn't have known it if Mr. Sterling hadn't waved his hands in the air. "Time for a break," he called, motioning her to the sidelines.

She flew across the ice to him.

"Good, clean skating this afternoon." He leaned on the railing that circled the rink.

"Thanks." She was surprised to see that he'd abandoned his bench. And glancing back, she realized that half of her audience was missing. "Too bad Mrs. Newton couldn't stay around."

He nodded. "Oh, but she saw some splendid moves before she returned to work."

The playful flicker in his eye made Livvy wonder why Mrs. Newton had *really* come.

She took a quick drink from her water bottle.

"Olivia . . . I want to talk to you about something."

She couldn't help but chuckle. "Do you have some more suggestions for me?"

He pulled out his note pad, grinning. "What do you say I give you a few pointers?"

"That all depends on how much you charge."

He reached for his pen. "We'll settle that little issue later."

"You used to coach some of the very best skaters back east, didn't you?"

His eyebrows flew up and hovered over his pensive blue eyes. "You've done your homework on me, I see."

"I sure did. I called Elena, my former coach, and she told me all about you."

"Well, well. You've discovered my secret."

"So you *have* to charge me," she insisted. "As well-known as Coach Odell Sterling is—"

"*Was,*" he said with a wink. "I'm hiding out in Podunk, remember?"

"Alpine Lake is the place to be."

"Thanks to you, Her Grace. Now . . . don't breathe a word, or I won't have much of a retirement, will I?"

"I *have* to tell my father. And my best friend and . . ."

He shook his head, chuckling. "Really, Livvy. I'm doing this for you. Only you."

"You're too good to be true, Mr. Sterling."

His eyes narrowed, and he put his hand on her shoulder.

Just like Elena used to. "I believe in you, Olivia."

"My mother used to say that."

He was nodding. "She had every reason to."

Livvy's heart was full of joy.

Jenna stopped by later, and Livvy introduced her to Odell Sterling. "He's a famous skating coach," she said. "But we can't tell anyone."

"Coming out of retirement on behalf of a talented young lady," he added, flashing an endearing smile Livvy's way.

"Can you believe it?" She was jumping up and down. "I've finally got myself a coach."

"What'll your dad say?" Jenna asked.

"What *can* he say?" Livvy said, settling down. "He'll be surprised, but I think I can talk him into it. After all, my grandma's running the show now. She'll help convince him."

"She's staying?" Jenna asked.

"Hey, she makes a mean pasta casserole, so I'm not complaining."

There was laughter all around.

Livvy said good-bye to Coach Sterling and promised to be prompt for their first real practice.

Tomorrow!

The girls walked down Main Street together. "This is so cool, Livvy," her friend said. "I'm so happy for you!"

"Yes, and I have a funny feeling you're partly responsible."

Jenna's lips pinched into a weird, almost mysterious expression. "My secret is sealed!"

"Wait a minute . . . that's what Mrs. Newton said about the cheerleading outfits." She stopped Jenna right there on the sidewalk. "She was in on this, wasn't she? She put a bug in Mr. Sterling's ear about me, didn't she?"

"What bug? And who are you talking about?" Jenna said ever so innocently.

"You talked to Mrs. Newton, and she told Mr. Sterling about my skating dreams. She must've known he was a retired skating coach—one of the best!"

"My lips are still sealed!" Jenna burst out laughing.

"See . . . I was right!"

But Jenna wouldn't admit it. "Mrs. Newton has some jazzy-looking patterns for skate costumes."

"You're changing the subject."

"Well, she *does*. And you'd better check them out."

Livvy flipped her hair. "I will when my grandma and I finish sewing Diane's cheerleading outfit."

"You must be kidding! *You're* sewing it?" Jenna slapped her forehead. "Does Diane know?"

"It's my secret . . . mine and Mrs. Newton's."

Jenna giggled. "And now it's ours." They walked another long block, chattering like gabby parrots.

"I know another secret," Jenna piped up, halfway to her house. "It's about Diane Larson. How do you think she knows so much about everyone?"

Livvy was laughing now. "Must be the school secretary—something about her reminds me of Diane."

"She's Diane's nosy aunt, who gets the scoop on everyone at the beginning of the year, then yaks it to Diane."

"So . . . *that's* how Diane knew I was a skater," said Livvy.

"Among other things." Jenna smiled her sweet, forgiving smile. "I don't know about you, but it's really no big deal to me . . . the gossip and stuff."

"I'm not surprised. You overlook everything."

"I try."

"Tell me about it." Livvy linked arms with her best friend.

Livvy's world was beginning to spin on its axis once again. She wouldn't be sitting alone at lunch anymore. Wouldn't be writing long, letter-type essays for Mrs. Smith. And she wouldn't be so grumpy to her parrot, either!

She was getting her confidence back, thanks to a lot of super folks. In a not-so-Podunk place!

"Do you think Mom has any idea about my new coach?" Livvy asked her dad before bedtime.

"Well, if she doesn't, I'd be surprised." He leaned down and kissed her forehead, tucking her in. "Good night, Livvy."

"I love you," she said. "Don't work too late."

"That's impossible." He shrugged helplessly.

"I know." She understood his motivation and drive. It

was the same kind of energy that inspired her to beat the sun up every morning.

Before turning out the light, her dad said, "Grandma's planning a big breakfast tomorrow. Better set your alarm."

"Oh, I'll be up. Easy."

"So will I," he said.

"Daddy?" She sat up in bed, staring across the room. "Does this mean what I think it does?"

He leaned on the door, his eyes serious. "It's time I met my daughter's coach."

"You're kidding . . . really?"

"Most of all, I want to see you skate, kiddo. I've missed out on too much . . . for too long."

It was impossible to sleep. An invisible choir of crickets buzzed away. The moon played tag with the bedroom curtains as they drifted back and forth. And Livvy daydreamed of regional competitions and ice revues.

Soon to come. . . .

Lying in the stillness, she began to whisper to her mother about all the super things that had happened since she'd moved to Alpine Lake. Things like getting a free (for now) top-notch coach. Like having a true friend named Jenna Song.

But she stopped. "Sorry, Mom. I'm not so sure I'm talking to the right person."

Livvy turned her chatter into a long prayer—and felt super good about it.

*Don't miss a single book
in the exciting* GIRLS ONLY *(GO!) series!*

#2: ONLY THE BEST

Jenna Song is thrilled when she's made captain of her gymnastics team. But she's having trouble with her aerial cartwheels—and the fall meet is only two weeks away! News of her parents' approval for a foreign adoption causes more distraction for Jenna as she struggles with feelings of jealousy. And she must choose between attending the gymnastics competition and going with her parents to bring home her new brother-to-be.

Will her best friend—Livvy Hudson—help her deal with her fears? Can Jenna learn to love and accept the baby boy who seems to threaten all her athletic goals and dreams?

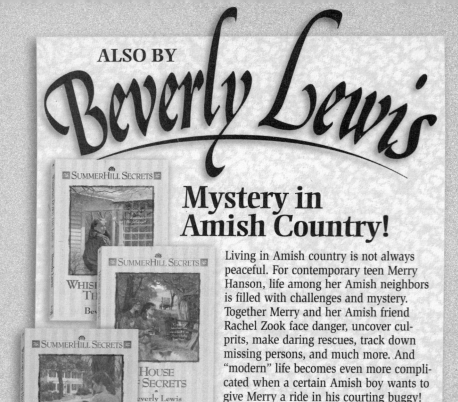

Also by Beverly Lewis

PICTURE BOOK
Cows in the House

THE CUL-DE-SAC KIDS
Children's Fiction

SUMMERHILL SECRETS
Youth Fiction

HOLLY'S HEART SERIES
Youth Fiction

THE HERITAGE OF LANCASTER COUNTY
Adult Fiction

OTHER ADULT FICTION
The Postcard
The Crossroad

The Sunroom

Series for Middle Graders* From BHP

ADVENTURES DOWN UNDER · by Robert Elmer
When Patrick McWaid's father is unjustly sent to Australia as a prisoner in 1867, the rest of the family follows, uncovering action-packed mystery along the way.

ADVENTURES OF THE NORTHWOODS · by Lois Walfrid Johnson
Kate O'Connell and her stepbrother Anders encounter mystery and adventure in northwest Wisconsin near the turn of the century.

AN AMERICAN ADVENTURE SERIES · by Lee Roddy
Hildy Corrigan and her family must overcome danger and hardship during the Great Depression as they search for a "forever home."

BLOODHOUNDS, INC. · by Bill Myers
Hilarious, hair-raising suspense follows brother-and-sister detectives Sean and Melissa Hunter in these madcap mysteries with a message.

GIRLS ONLY! · by Beverly Lewis
Four talented young athletes become fast friends as together they pursue their Olympic dreams.

JOURNEYS TO FAYRAH · by Bill Myers
Join Denise, Nathan, and Josh on amazing journeys as they discover the wonders and lessons of the mystical Kingdom of Fayrah.

MANDIE BOOKS · by Lois Gladys Leppard
With over four million sold, the turn-of-the-century adventures of Mandie and her many friends will keep readers eager for more.

THE RIVERBOAT ADVENTURES · by Lois Walfrid Johnson
Libby Norstad and her friend Caleb face the challenges and risks of working with the Underground Railroad during the mid–1800s.

TRAILBLAZER BOOKS · by Dave and Neta Jackson
Follow the exciting lives of real-life Christian heroes through the eyes of child characters as they share their faith with others around the world.

THE TWELVE CANDLES CLUB · by Elaine L. Schulte
When four twelve-year-old girls set up a business of odd jobs and baby-sitting, they uncover wacky adventures and hilarious surprises.

THE YOUNG UNDERGROUND · by Robert Elmer
Peter and Elise Andersen's plots to protect their friends and themselves from Nazi soldiers in World War II Denmark guarantee fast-paced action and suspenseful reads.

*(ages 8–13)